Blackout

Blackout

Magdalina Goranova

Magdalina Goranova
2019

Acknowledgements

First off, I would like to thank the authors Marissa Meyer and Stephenie Meyer for their wonderful books which gave me inspiration and ideas throughout my writing process. Without all these amazing books, I would probably still be writing Chapter One.

I am extremely grateful to my friend Caleigh Douglas for helping me design the front cover and being my editor from the very beginning.

Deep appreciation to my friends Nina Nemcanin, Leila Nelson, and my dear brother Kristian Goranov whose use of the editor's red pen helped improve the book by a lot.

Special thanks to my teachers- Mrs. Eagan, Ms. Mcclanahan, and Ms. Oyler for helping me edit and publish this book.

Love and endless gratitude to my parents who were always there, supporting me.

All my thanks to everyone who has helped me and supported me throughout this adventure. I really appreciate all your help.

August 2100 (81 years from 2019)

Luna Russell

Everything was cold. And dark. Unfriendly and hostile.
This was Earth without the Sun.

"Courtney, can you please run down to the Nutri?"

"You go! I'm not going out there. I might miss my date!" my older sister yelled back. She was always thinking about her boyfriend Kian, her looks, and other things sixteen-year-old girls would think about. That, I couldn't understand.

The Sun hadn't shown up in a week. I was concerned about the safety of humans and what would happen to Earth itself. Humankind had reached it's lowest point of existence. We no longer had any animals to keep our planet alive. The whole animal kingdom that once roamed the planet were all gone. Wiped off the face of the Earth because of the stupidity and greed that humankind carried with them. It was the same with the trees, flowers and plants. All over our planet. For many years people wanted more money and more power. All that lead to ruthless pollution that ended up plaguing our planet.

We no longer had fresh water sources. Instead, every household had a special machine that was able to convert ocean water into alkalized, ionized, electrolyzed drinking water. Food was no longer available, as well. The Imperium government approved Nutritional pills (Nutri) for consumption that they claim to be providing us with enough vitamins, minerals, and nutrients to help our bodies function properly. However, I doubted this. I watched as everyone turned to skin and bones. There were no more obese people. We were all malnourished.

Most people were in a desperate financial situation. The world population decreased to only a couple of billion people due to no water and no food. Many people did not survive, others lost their sanity, some even committed suicide.

All the greed for money and power the soulless corporations had forced them to create more and more products that endangered the wellbeing of our planet. This made Earth a living dumpster. Because of all the pollution we lost animals, plants, food, water, and now the Sun.

Mom. I was really worried about mom.

Audrey Russell, our mom, worked for NASA. Ever since the Sun disappeared well, let's say she was too busy with work to come home.

As for our dad. . . we lost him in the Third World War. I never knew who he was. He died when I was eight months old. Most kids' parents do. Or did. Whatever you prefer.

I was only fourteen, the youngest in my family.

I had two siblings, twins. Courtney and Dominik were both jerks. When mom was around, they acted like angels in order for her to let them buy the latest robot or the latest technology in general. They had many, and were spoiled brats. They disposed of their old stuff one after another in what they called "accidents". Childish business.

I remember when Supreme Homework Buster Robot 2.6 came out. My brother Dominik, had had the Mega Homework Buster Robot 1.0 and thought that he needed the new edition. I saw no difference between them. Both helped you with homework. Dominik threw his Homework Buster off the roof of Wood's High School. He said it must've been an accident. But I knew better.

Nevertheless, he did get the new robot.

Robots are awful. Like seriously. Why do you need robots to help you with homework when you have a brain in your head? Why? I'll bet you anything robots will take over the world. Maybe robots are behind the Sun, disappearing. Maybe. Or maybe not.

There were many theories behind *this*.

Some said it was an alien invasion.

Others said the devil was upon us.

Nonsense.

This could be explained by science. It had to be. Everything else was.

Science was the subject of the Earth. Literally. Science explains everything around you. Leaves are green because of photosynthesis. Science. Atomic bombs explode because someone is separating atoms. Science. We were shielded from ultraviolet radiation because of the ozone layer. Well, before. The ozone layer hardly exists nowadays. But still, *science*.

I was sure science could explain this catastrophe.

It had to.

But whatever was happening, scientists and astronomers were taking a long time figuring it out. The temperature was dropping a couple of degrees every day. It was 24 degrees Fahrenheit today, but yesterday it was 26. Not good. Definitely not good.

I was out there, a lot. Too much. I went out to buy breakfast, lunch, and heating supplies. I went out to buy lamps. And gasoline. And lots of other stuff. Couldn't I stay in for a while?

Ever since mom ran off to the laboratory, Courtney and Dominik have been treating me horribly. Like I'm responsible for feeding them and all the other things.

"Courtney, unless you go get some Nutri, there will be no dinner!"

"Don't then, no one's making you."

"Okay, that's it. I'm going outside. I need to know what's happening. Dr. Marcy Brown's press conference should be starting any moment, now."

Courtney came to the hallway, blocking the doorway. She had changed since I last saw her. She now wore a red sweater that perfectly outlined her curves. I could never look that good in a big, fluffy sweater. Her blonde hair was in curls that gently bounced against the sides of her face. She had the skinniest jeans and I wondered how she could sit without them splitting open.

Truth be told, that would be quite funny.

"You're not going anywhere. It's cold, and I'm hungry. Everything will be okay. Before you know it, the Sun will come out again." she said, brushing her hair to one side. I, unlike her, did not have perfect dimples and perfect hair. I was made of imperfections. I had the lightest brown hair you could imagine. It wasn't blonde but it wasn't the dark brown most people have. It wasn't dirty blonde, either. My face did not have the princess-look my sister owned. I wore a flannel shirt and fuzzy leggings. I had teal sneakers that gave me no warmth and protection whatsoever.

"Was that supposed to be for moral support? You know, I'm not a child anymore. You know I can't believe that. Why waste your words?" I said, squeezing by her, "I'm going out there. I need to know."

"No, you're not. Everything will be alright," said Dominik. I hadn't noticed him inching toward us. "You know it will."

"No, it won't. You're fools to believe that!" I said, getting my coat and heading toward the door. "The Sun hasn't come out in a week! Something bad may be happening!" I put my coat on but my brother pulled me back by my hair.

"You're not going anywhere! What don't you understand, Luna?!? You can't go out there!"

"I don't understand why you guys can hang out and can go out of the house for dates, and I can't go out to see a press conference. For all I know, mom might be there!" I growled. "OW! Let me go!"

"Alright, you win. If you die, I don't care."

I snarled at him, then opened the door and left the house. Courtney and Dominik didn't see me as a sister, they saw me as a replacement mom. What the heck?

I ventured through Mulberry Street,and yes, you heard me right. Our street was named after the legendary Dr. Seuss and his first book, *And To Think That I Saw It On Mulberry Street*.

Everything was covered in ice and snow. For once, I wished I had my hat with me. That useless hat hadn't come to use at all and I didn't think I would need it. I mean, we lived in Miami. It was hot, very hot. Most of the days at least. 70 years ago Miami was a big city, but due to water levels rising, the shoresides of the city were flooded and swallowed by Mother Nature.

I looked up to the dark night sky, hoping to catch some sign that the sun was coming out. Nope. I saw the same endless sky littered with the same stars and galaxies. There was no moon. No moon, no sun. What was going on?

My watch read 3:23 P.M.

It should have been light, warm, and sunny.

It wasn't, though, and I was about to find out why.

When I reached Jackson Hall, it was already 3:36. I was late. I didn't think the cold weather would hold me up with six minutes. I found a seat in the back and sat down. I was crammed between two jumpy journalists but I made no objections. At least I was here.

Dr. Marcy Brown had already stepped onto the podium. She wore a blue sweater with some design I couldn't quite make out from the back. Her sweatpants matched her sweater. Dr. Marcy Brown had her usual wet cherry red hair splattered across the side of her face. Although I couldn't see her that clearly from here, I could tell she hadn't had a good night's sleep in a long time.

Dr. Marcy Brown continued her speech, before pausing so the eager journalists could ask their questions.

A journalist stood up. He wore green khakis and a blue Polo shirt. He had black hair, but his back was facing me, so I couldn't exactly make out his features.

"Dr. Marcy Brown, what is happening with the Sun? Why isn't it showing up?" he asked, his voice full of urgency. He spoke in what seemed to be an Armenian accent, but I wasn't quite sure. I focused on the question he'd asked, instead. Everyone wanted to know the answer to that question.

Everyone.

Including me.

"Uh, yes. About that, as you already know, scientists have confirmed that the Sun was a star. You know, back in 450 BCE. Well, as we all know, once a star dies, it turns into a black hole. The Sun has died and is now a. . . black hole. This is why we no longer have a Sun." she said, emphasizing every word.

Gasps filled the room.

The Sun.

It was gone.

There was no Sun, just a black hole in its place.

"Dr. Marcy Brown, can you please tell us more about the process of a star dying and becoming a black hole?" asked a young journalist, a little older than Courtney.

Courtney. How I despised her right now. She could go out and about and I couldn't. I despised everything about that. I was being childish and I knew it. I had to be stronger. The world was going to meet its doom quite soon. I needed to help them.

"Yes, of course. When the core of a star runs out of hydrogen fuel, it will contract under the weight of the gravity. The upper layers of the star will expand and eject material that will collect around the dying star to form a planetary nebula. Then, the core will cool and become a white dwarf. Later, the star will become a black dwarf and then become a black hole. In the case of the sun, it merely exploded and turned into a black hole. It skipped some phases." she explained. "The explosion of the Sun we know as the *Tempus Arindam* of 2020-2044. During that time the average temperature rose and Earth suffered severe droughts. Since then, the Sun has slowly evolved into the black hole we know it is today." Dr. Marcy Brown said. "We humans speeded up this process by polluting our planet. All toxic gases, plastic waste, and radiation played a key role in extinguishing the Sun quicker than predicted."

Panic started flowing into the room, like a contagious virus out on the loose. People were jumping out of their seats, elbowing their way out of the room. Like that could help us. Everyone was panicking their faces controlled by fear. The smirk on my face though, couldn't hide my true emotions. I was scared. Really scared.

"What are we going to do?" wailed a journalist.

"The Sun gave Earth the gravity it needed to stay in our solar system. To stay in orbit, and now that it's gone, we have started to float away into space. In order for humankind to survive we must leave Earth immediately." said Dr. Marcy Brown, in a calm casual way. It wasn't even the way you'd say *'Sup?* It was very diplomatic.

I was suddenly aware of myself. I was aware of my sweaty palms rubbing against each other in anxiety. I was aware of my feet tapping the floor in nervous taps. I was aware of my breathing and how it sped up with the idea of moving to another planet

Another planet.

Possibly another galaxy.

Another home.

Oh my goodness, we were abandoning Earth!

"Starting right now, please pack all the necessary items that you'll need. You may not pack anything more than 100 pounds. Please return to your homes immediately. I repeat, please return to your homes immediately," ordered Dr. Marcy Brown.

I turned to the door, not waiting to hear anything else. I needed to get out of here. Mom would come home soon. I needed to get out of here before everyone decided to get out. I headed toward the door, opened it but was met by a bulky man. The muscles on his chest were visible through his grey sweater. He wore khaki-colored trousers, that were an inch too short.

Trousers. Those were old fashioned.

"You must be Professor Audrey Russell's daughter. She asked for you to meet her in the lab room."

Luna Russell

"My name is Abbyson Gullery. I work for your mom. I'm her guard. I've heard many things about you, Luna. Your mom said that you'll possibly make it to NASA, one day." said Abbyson, as he marched down the crowded aisle. "Hey, move it! Anyway, Audrey's a sweet woman. Kind, ambitious, supportive. . . what more could you want? Do you have siblings? Your mom didn't mention that. All she talks about is you and your talent."

I frowned.

I didn't remember my mom being that fond of me, because she usually favored Courtney and Dominik. And I certainly haven't heard about whatever is going on between my mom and this Abbyson Gullery.

Abbyson Gullery led me through the back of the stage and up some stairs. Everything smelled like metal, but not in a good way. We turned right and found ourselves in a vast lab room.

Facing me was a desk with messy papers, paperclips, and other things scattered across the desk. A telescope was near it. The carpeted floor muffled my footsteps, but otherwise, I was sure you could hear my heart beating through my feet. Everything was so big and massive. So many instruments. I spotted sextants, microscopes, and armillary spheres. To my left, a large window covered most of the wall. I supposed they used it for stargazing. To my right were a couple lab tables with dents and stains all over them. Everything was so . . . amazing. Right away I knew that I would want to work in this kind of environment when I grew up.

"Luna, sit down. Abbyson, you can leave her to me." said a familiar voice. I hadn't noticed my mom emerging from behind one of the tanks.

"Whatever you say, Madame Russell."

Madame Russell?

As far as I knew, my mom hated being called formal names. I looked back at my mom. She showed no signs of her dislike in formal names. Confusion started creeping up inside me, but I pushed it down. Instead, I decided to fill myself with awe and admiration.

"Mom, why did you call for me?" I asked, once the guard was out of the room. "Courtney and Dominik have no idea about the 'another planet thing'. I have to go back home."

"Of course, you do. You're my responsible little butterfly." she said, inching toward me; her arms spread open. Was I supposed to hug her? She came closer to me and wrapped her arms around me. I let the hug be for a moment or so and then pushed away.

"Mom, that wasn't a compliment, was it? Butterflies are extinct." I said, backing up by the wall. "Anyway, tell me what you wanted to tell me."

"We must move to another planet. I know you know that but the astronomers and the cosmologists, they don't know what planet we're going to. We're basically going to pack up people in a spaceship and go off into nowhere."

"Mom, why are you telling me this?"

"Because I have to stay on Earth. Someone has to control the spaceship and send coordinates." she said, worry snagging at every word she spoke.

The world around me whirled and I became numb as if someone just gave me a numbing shot.

My mom was going to die. For the sake of humanity.

She was going to die.

Going to die.

Die.

Everything echoed in my head and nothing made any sense.

Why?

Why her?

"Luna. Luna!" she snapped at me. "You're going to be fine. You've took such good care of Courtney and Dominik I can trust you. That's why I'm doing this."

"You can't do this, though! Not after what we've been through. Remember when our home burned down? We stayed together. When you lost your job at the Astro-Cosmology center? We stayed together? Why are we splitting up now?"

"Because it's my job and my duty. You'll do good without me. Courtney and Dominik can take care of themselves. Now run off, and pack your bags. Send Dominik and Courtney my everlasting love. Now go."

She pushed me out of the door. I let her. I was numb. I couldn't focus on my thoughts. Everything was a blur and I couldn't think straight. Before I could say a proper goodbye, she'd pushed me out onto the snowy streets, shutting the door behind her.

I didn't want to go, but I did. I ran toward our house, ignoring everyone, sobbing until the words felt hollow.

Mom wouldn't come to the other planet with us.

She would die.

As would the rest of the human population, probably.

Most likely.

I opened the door to our house and flung myself inside.

Luna Russell

"What's wrong with you?" yelled Dominik, his girlfriend tugging at his waist.

"Come on, let's go back to your room. I'm freezing." pleaded his girlfriend in a high pitched squeaky voice.

"Well, no duh. You're in a tank top and leggings." said Courtney, rising from off the couch.

"Pack your bags. We're going to leave Earth soon. Mom's not coming with us." I said. "And shut your mouth, Dominik. I was not wailing, I simply yelped."

"Is that why you're crying?" asked Dominik, his eyebrow curiously raising.

"I wasn't crying. I yelped. I already told you that. My hair got stuck, when the door was closing, " I said, rubbing my scalp. "Pack your bags, now. What's your name?"

My brother's girlfriend looked at me in a curious manner. "Whitney. Whitney Stone." said his girlfriend, straightening up. "My parents are part of the Astronomical Research Team. You might know them, Amanda and Jerry Stone. That's how I met Dominik, here."

"Good. You of all people should know, that we're in terrible danger. Go home and pack your bags."

"I won't be bossed around by some *kid*. I'll stay here with my sweetheart," squeaked Whitney, cuddling with Dominik even more.

"Okay." I said, trying to process all the thoughts that were going through my brain. "Dominik, why don't you go to Whitney's house to help her pack? This way Whitney won't be alone."

"Sure, why not?" said Dominik, picking up Whitney and kissing her.

"Courtney, pack your bags."

"But Kian will be here any moment," complained Courtney. "It would be so humiliating if I missed my date."

I sighed, ignoring the last comment.

"Kian who? Is that your boyfriend?"

"Kian Sparks. He's the cool boy in my class. He asked me out and I said yes."

"Cool. You know what? I bet he'll think you're really smart when you're packing up for this trip," I said in a grown-up way. "When he comes, I'll send him right up to your room. Is that fine?"

"Sure," mumbled Courtney, heading up to her room. "But you better tell me, or else . . ."

I sighed.

I felt like a policeman. Or policewoman.

You do this. You do that.

I didn't like it but when your *older* siblings act like they're younger than you, you have to redirect them. I spun around and headed up the stairs.

"Right, see you later, babe." I said, putting the phone down. Luna had been gone almost an hour. Could the press conference be that long?

I heard a knock.

I turned to the door. If it was Luna, she would open it herself. Who was it, then? I opened the door to find a girl about my age staring at me. Not Luna. Definitely not Luna.

The girl had pitch black curly hair that flowed like a river over her shoulders. She had a round face, but was skinny. She had pitch black eyes that projected kindness. She had a puffy purple jacket and black skinny jeans. Brown high-heeled boots finished her look.

"Hi! I'm Whitney. Whitney Stone- Dominik's girlfriend," she said happily.

"Of course you are. He has a new one every week," I said, letting her in.

"He does? Hmm. Well he swore to me that he loves me, and me only." she said. I was 100% sure she was trying to convince herself more than convince me.

"His room is upstairs, the second one on your left."

Whitney happily bounced up the stairs. Poor girl. Dominik was just going to take advantage of her and her beauty, but I couldn't do anything about it. I went over to the couch and flopped down onto it. My Make-o-Bot came into the room, her treds moving as she came closer and closer to me.

"Master Courtney, I have made your mascara order. I speculate it will be here in 3 days." said the Make-o-Bot in its depressing monotone voice.

"Make-o-Bot, send me Luna Russell's coordinates." I ordered. Seconds later I got a text.

From: Make-o-Bot: Luna Russell's coordinates

12,48
Jackson Street, Miami, Imperium.

Stupid, stupid, stupid me. Of course, she was still at the press conference. Thank goodness the government manufactured small identity chips to put in one's wrist. I just needed to make sure that she was there, that she was okay. Although it didn't seem like I cared for her much from the side, she was the dearest thing that happened to me. I couldn't bear lose her. Not after we lost Dad.

"Master Courtney, Master Dominik calls me. May I go- hnfs- nfsr- upstairs to assist him?"

Stupid glitches.

"I grant you full permission."

My eyes followed Make-o-Bot upstairs. My eyes fell back on the text.

Imperium.

Not long ago we had the Third World War. Afterwards, all the world leaders decided to make one big country to ensure peace. *Imperium.* It meant power in Latin. Not that we had any power after the war. I think the government was trying to get us motivated to do great things, and truth to be told, that didn't work out.

People were powerless. During the elections, they said our votes counted but, I knew better. Our votes were nothing but lies. Lies, lies, lies. Imperium, the country based off of lies. Every person on the planet, telling lies to keep their darkest secrets from being undercovered. Every person, forging their own protective mask, to keep themselves hidden.

Every person.

Including me.

Including Dominik.

Including mom.

And dad when he was alive.

Everyone except Luna.

She was open and had nothing to hide.

Nothing.

That's why I admire her so much. That's why I love her so dearly, although I hide it behind my lies. Behind my mask.

She wasn't made of lies.

She had nothing to hide. Unlike all of us. Unlike me. Unlike the stranger running down the street. Unlike my math teacher Mrs. Jones. Lies, lies, lies. A world of lies.

4 minutes earlier
Dominik Russell

"Hey Dominik," said a familiar voice. I spun around, leaving my unfinished homework. It was Whitney. I was mesmerized by her every time. "Whatcha doin'?"

"Nothing much, just finishing some history. Did you do the timeline of human accomplishments?" I asked, keeping an eye on her. She casually sat down on the floor. "I'm on 2019 and I can't seem to remember what happened then."

"I'm at 1816, you know, when they made the first camera." she said.

I laughed, and got up.

Whitney laughed with me and slowly took off her winter coat, emphasizing every movement.

"Can we work on the project?" asked Whitney.

I heard the front door open, and then a cry. Could it be my annoying little sister? Nah. But if it wasn't her, who would it be?

I stepped away from Whitney.

"Whitney, I have to go downstairs to see who it is. I'll be right back."

"But your sister's down there." pouted Whitney. "And we haven't even started on the project yet."

"Then come with me. It'll be quick."

We went downstairs, Whitney tugging at my waist the whole time. There was Luna, standing in the doorway, rubbing her scalp.

"What's wrong with you?" I yelled. I was pissed. She ruined my fun. Though working on the stupid project wouldn't be *that* fun.

Luna said something about mom not coming, that we had to evacuate or something. I could care less about this astronomical business, but I could sense Whitney's arms tightening around me with every word Luna said. She was scared. Maybe I didn't care about Luna and outer space, but I sure cared about Whitney. Luna was right about one thing, I would go to Whitney's house and help her pack. That way she'll have me for support.

We ventured on upstairs and I helped Whitney put on her coat. She was scared, I could tell, because she'd gone all blank and had started to tremble. Once we were done, I helped her go downstairs, carefully guiding her so that she wouldn't miss a stair. The freezing air slapped me in the face as soon as I opened the door, making a foreign sound escape through my teeth.

Stupid Luna and her astronomical business. Stupid mom and *her* astronomical business. Stupid Courtney and her snide comments. Stupid dad for going into some war and leaving us all broke. Stupid Imperium and its dumb laws. Stupid world and its stupid people (excluding Whitney and I). Stupid Sun and its inability to function properly. Stupid. Stupid. Stupid.

The world was stupid.

Present

Luna Russell

I spun around and opened the door that lead to the basement. A cold breeze greeted me. Surely I wouldn't spend that much time packing up. I didn't own many things. I headed downstairs and flopped myself onto the old mattress. I never had a room, not even in our old house. I always got the basement. I didn't mind, though. It was larger than my siblings' rooms and the heater worked almost all the time. I got up and looked for things to pack. Clothes. Telescopes. My holographic encyclopedia.

I looked at my silver nail polish gleaming at me. It twinkled as if saying, *Everything will be alright! Just stay happy and be on the positive side of life!*

Which was kind of hard to do when everything around you was dark, cold, and gloomy.

I liked it though.

It reminded me of the moon and how it gleamed at Earth at night. Of the stars that littered the sky. I went over by the makeshift closet and rummaged for things to put my luggage in.

Aha! A grey suitcase and two silver duffle bags.

Perfect.

I gathered all my clothes and put them in one of the duffle bags. As I said, I didn't own much. My hair brush, dental devices, and other stuff went into the second duffle bag. Afterwards, I loaded all my telescopes, my microscope, protractors, and Armillary spheres in my suitcase.

I looked around once more. The only thing, I would be leaving would be the mattress.

Oh, gosh dang it!

I had forgotten all my tablets containing my school work. I rummaged through the closet, hoping to find a another suitcase or duffle bag.

Nope.

I would have to ask Courtney for one. I looked around the room one last time, my eyes setting upon the clock mom had gotten me. It was black and instead of numbers, there were the phases of the moon. I heaved a sigh, as I reached for the clock. I would take that as well. Maybe shove it into the suitcase.

I turned around and started up the stairs. Once I got up to the main floor, I was relieved to be out of the cold. Sure, my heaters worked. Sometimes. Up here, the heaters worked nonstop. Goodness, one day the heaters may explode because of overworking. I climbed the stairs carefully, keeping my balance for fear of dumping Cassie on the ground.

"Hey Courtney, do you have a duffel bag or suitcase I could borrow?" I yelled, reaching the top of the stairs. I turned the corner and walked toward her room. Courtney stuck her head out of the doorway.

"Yes, but not for you." said Courtney, smirking. "You could borrow one of Dominik's suitcases."

"C'mon, Courtney, have a heart." I pleaded, walking to her room. "I have my tablets to pack. Plus, I'll probably find some moldy Nutri in Dominik's duffle bags."

"Luna, who cares about school?" she said, rolling her eyes at me. "Fine, whatever. You can have the navy green duffle bag. It's somewhere in my closet."

"Thank you, thank you, thank you!" I squealed, running into her room.

"Luna, what the heck?" asked Courtney in her usual mocking tone. The tone I hated. Somehow, Courtney always found something to make fun of me. "Ah, you're pathetic."

I stood up, growling at Courtney. When was she going to learn that we are all different? That not everyone was the average Imperium citizen.

I headed over toward the closet. After rummaging for a while, the bag finally emerged from its hiding place.

"Have you thought of changing yourself?" asked Courtney, smirking at me. I looked at her, questions and snide comments popping up in my mind. Courtney, on the other hand, was folding her clothes and putting them into a glittery pink suitcase. "You know, things might be different if you do."

"Courtney, what are you trying to tell me?" I asked, rising from the floor and heading toward her. "Spit it out."

Courtney sighed, looking at me. It looked almost as if she was about to laugh.

"Nothing, I was just playing with you." she said, in a playful tone that drove me to the last of my nerves.

"No, you're not. You really want me to change." I said, rising from the bed. "I'm not stupid, Courtney. Tell me what I have to change"

"I said you don't have to change. I told you I was messing with you. What don't you understand, baby sister?"

"Courtney, stop. You know I despise that name. Don't call me it. Please." I pleaded, heading toward the duffle bag. "Now, if you'll excuse me, I need to get packing. And in case you haven't noticed, we'll be moving to another planet later today."

And with that, I exited the room, slamming the door behind me.

Dr. Marcy Brown

"Is the Urania 2.7 completed? Does it have all the necessary things to support the human race for an extended period of time? And have you found out where the increased supply of food came from?" I asked, moving through the brightly lit, sterile hallway. I severely disliked how everything was so white. The light bulbs gave off too much light for me. Why couldn't we just have more windows and use the Sun for light? But alas, the sun didn't exist anymore. As if reading my mind, Professor Audrey Russell spoke.

"I know, the light bulbs weren't the best choice but they were our only choice. Now with the Sun gone, things have been tough." she said, gripping the pile of documentary folders tightly in order to prevent them from splattering on the ground in an un-orderly mess. "As to answer your question, yes, the Urania 2.7 has the necessary things to support human life. I'm afraid humans will have to leave behind their robots. We won't have enough electricity to power them all and stay afloat in outer space. We have enough food and other supplies. Detectives Shaw Edinburgh and Lavender Bones have not found out where the food came from. Apart from that, everything is all set."

"Oh, great. Try to hustle up the process of filtration. We need to leave as quickly as possible. And are we going to take prisoners with us? Leonora didn't tell me anything useful about that matter." I said, squeezing my sweaty palms together.

"Do you mean Dr. Leonora Peterson from the fourth floor?"

"Yes, that's right."

"Well, she was quite unsure about the matter so she decided to let you make the decision. Most of the research team agrees on leaving them on Earth."

I looked at Audrey, horrified to hear this. How could you leave human beings on Earth? That's like ordering a death sentence. That's like leaving the third-class prisoners on the Titanic. I felt a surge of pain in my chest as I remembered that moment I read about it, and that one moment that I watched the historic movie about the sinking of the Titanic. This is what we had done to Earth. Left it to while away in space, like the third-class passengers, when they were locked and forced to die. And humans were the first class passengers, who got top priority of everything. How sad. But I knew that we had no time to think about this. We needed to leave Earth, now.

"Leave them on Earth?" I asked, unable to keep the disgust out of my voice. "Audrey, what do you think of this?"

"I think they should stay." explained Audrey. She showed no feeling, just kept on walking. "With so many people on board, the prisoners could cause havoc and panic. You know some of them are murderers. It'll be like putting sheep in the middle of a wolf pack."

"Audrey, I thought you were sensitive!" I exclaimed. "It's unfair! They're humans too!"

"Remember that I'll be staying on Earth as well. I'll be getting that death sentence, too," explained Audrey. Her voice sounded bitter as if she was unhappy with her staying here.

"Audrey, you volunteered to stay. You have kids and you volunteered to stay." I protested, every bitter feeling clawing at my throat. "How can you say this?"

"I don't know, I just can't." she said. This was so sketchy. She was faceless. She showed no feeling whatsoever. As if she was wearing a mask of some sort. "Dr. Brown, go home to your child. He'll be needing you. I'll make sure everything is in order. Go."

I hesitantly turned to Audrey, not able to make the decision of whether I should go to my family or if I should stay and make sure everything is properly done. Although we were friends of some sort, I didn't quite trust Audrey at the moment. Audrey nodded at me and made a walking hand motion. I sighed and sped down the corridor toward the gleaming green exit sign.

Dominik Russell

"C'mon, we need to hurry." I said as we sped down the street.

"Yeah, but it's freezing cold!" complained Whitney.

"Babe, remember that I have to pack my bags as well. Now what street did you live on, again?"

"Pulchra Street." replied Whitney, her breath coming out of her mouth as heavy mist.

"Pulchra. That's an unusual name?" I said, now practically running. "I'm guessing it's Latin, just like everything else in Imperium."

"Yes, it means beautiful in Latin."

"Is that why you're beautiful?" I said, attempting to make a flattering joke.

"No, silly." said Whitney with a laugh that filled my heart up with warm and fuzzy feelings. "I was born beautiful."

"Quite right,"

"Here," said Whitney. "This is my apartment building."

We stopped by a huge apartment building. I couldn't tell exactly what color it was but, it definitely blended in with the night sky. We stepped inside and headed toward the elevators.

"Only the best buildings could hold the best people." I said, as we stepped into the elevator. Jazz music played softly overhead and I was annoyed by it for unknown reasons.

"What's that supposed to mean?"

"It means that you're an amazing person, and this is an amazing building, so that's why you live in it." I explained, trying to block out the annoying music.

"I don't get it."

"Nevermind," I said, sighing. My attempt to make a flattering joke was obviously pathetic. So much for trying to be cool. The elevator jerked up, leaving my gut behind. Once the elevator stopped, we emerged into a shabby looking hallway.

It was painted baby blue but the paint was starting to peel away. The carpet was designed to look like a wood floor. It smelled of mold or something rotten. Mold was starting to creep up in the corners and the doors looked as if they were about to fall down. The light bulbs flickered on and off as if fighting for life. Whitney lead us to a similar looking door with the number 492 painted on it. She rummaged through her pockets and took out a large brass key. She pushed it through the keyhole and with lots of effort, opened the door.

"So, this is my home." she said, stepping inside as if it were paradise.

"It's nice," I said, trying to put false happiness in my voice. The place reeked of a strong perfume.

"I'll be in my room packing." she said, turning right down a small corridor and opening a door with the letter *W* painted in the middle of it with glittery purple paint. "Make yourself at home, babe."

Wow, it was amazing how she said all this with such ease. The furniture was old. There was no sign of a robot which, directly indicated that she was of fourth class.

In Imperium, the society was split into four classes. The President, his elite, other important members of the Ministry, and rich people were in first class. CEO people, managers, IT people, inventors, and scientists were in the second class. Teachers, soldiers, random employees in random companies, and other people like that were in the third class. Fourth class people were prisoners, criminals on the loose, maids, taxi drivers, janitors, and poor people were of the fourth class.

This was very strange, since Whitney claimed her parents were Amanda and Jerry Stone, cosmology experts on the NASA research team. She should have been in second class, like us, but she wasn't. Unless she was lying about her parents.

She *was* probably lying. Gosh, I was so stupid. Stupid, stupid, stupid me. How could I be dating a fourth class girl? Sure, she was pretty but she wasn't on my level.

I walked over to the door with the *W* and knocked.

"Come in, babe."

"Whitney, who are your parents, really? If you really were from second class, you would live in a nice house, like me. Who are your parents, really?" I said, pushing the door open and entering her room. It was a dark small space with only one light bulb hanging. Wires protruded from the top of the bulb making it look like a Christmas tree hanging upside down. A bed with pink covers sat on the left side of the room and directly parallel to it was a tiny wardrobe. The room contained no other furniture. It was tiny!

"Whitney, answer my question. Who are your real parents?"

"I. . . I can't tell you. You'll never speak to me again." mumbled Whitney. For a second, I took pity upon her but that quickly vanished.

"Whitney, tell me. I have a right to know."

Whitney sighed and then looked at me. Her eyes projected sadness.

"My parents are Ruby Cox and Ethan Ciapponi. You know, the world-famous murderers. I. . . I'm not proud of it. In fact, I'm ashamed of it. Please, don't split up with me because of that. I. . . I'm not like my parents." said Whitney. I could see tears springing up to her eyes. "I was a mistake. My parents were both mad at Felix Ramsey, the president at the time, and they decided to murder him. They worked together and nine months later, I was born. They didn't want me so they abandoned me on the streets. An elderly woman found me, an elderly lady, and decided to take care of me but . . . but . . . she died when I was four. Ever since, I've been taking care of myself."

Whitney was really crying now. I tried to wrap my arms around her, to comfort her, but she pushed me away.

"I know you really must hate me for lying to you, but I didn't have a choice! I was so . . . into you and I knew that you would never date me! I'm so sorry!"

"It . . . it's okay." I said, now trying desperately to comfort her. "But Whitney, you need to understand. I can't trust you. I don't know what you've got from . . . *them*. I've never seen anything bad come from you but, I can never be sure. I think it's best if we stay away from each other."

"But I love you! I'll never do anything to hurt you." wailed Whitney. "Don't go! Please!"

"I-" I couldn't finish. I would always remember her pretty face. I would always remember the amazing personality that made me feel complete for once. I would always remember Whitney, but we couldn't be together. It would be bad for my reputation. It would be bad for me. I turned and pushed the door open and exited into the rotten-smelling hallway.

"No! Stop, Dominik!" cried Whitney after me. I wouldn't stop. I couldn't stop. Nothing could stop me. Nothing. I had made the right decision. She was a bad person. A bad person who would do bad things for my reputation and for me. I couldn't stop. I wouldn't stop. Whitney was not right for me.

Whitney Stone

I flung myself onto the bed and cried. I cried until no tears could come out anymore. I cried until the true meaning of Dominik's departure had settled in. I cried until the words, *He's not coming back because of you*, became hollow. Dominik had dumped me. He'd just abandoned me. I had never done anything to hurt him. I had never planned on hurting him. Goodness, I loved him so much. He was my Moon, my Galaxy, my . . . Sun. But the Sun had turned into a black hole, just like Dominik's feelings toward me. I should've known. Idiotic Whitney, idiotic Whitney, idiotic Whitney! I should've known that because of my parentage, I had no future. I should've known that because of my parentage, no boy would permanently settle down with me once they knew the truth. I should've known that people would make judgements. That people would think I'm like my parents. But no. My head had been swayed by my love for Dominik.

Love. It was beautiful. It was art. It was everything I had always wanted. I had always wanted someone to love me, the public to love me, and . . . I had always wanted to love myself. But I couldn't. Love was also evil, cruel, and traumatizing.

Maybe not physically, but I carried scars. Scars from being dumped, from being abandoned, from every other negative feeling I had experienced.

Ever since, I went to an ancestry website to find out who my parents were, the world hated me. Once I found out, I even paid extra to keep the truth from being revealed to the public but no. The next day, my face was on every newspaper, on every phone, on every billboard. I had been registered as a wanted criminal, although I hadn't done anything. A sum of money was placed on my head so large, that you could've bought all of Africa with it. Well, what used to be Africa. By the next morning, everyone knew the name Tiffany Ciapponi. Everyone knew my name, so I changed it in hopes of creating a new life. In hopes of starting back at Chapter one. Whitney Stone. That would be my name in my new life. The government wanted me in jail because they were afraid of me.

Curse you, Whitney! Arghh, I had been so foolish, believing that I could ever be loved. Why couldn't I just be normal? *No one is normal*, I reminded myself. Everyone is obscured by lies. Everyone wears a mask. I had forged my own mask, making people believe that I was the daughter of Amanda and Jerry Stone. I had obscured myself in lies, but so had Dominik. What he revealed to me today taught me a great lesson.

Don't judge a book by it's cover. Wait for it.

Dominik had seemed so sweet, loving, and kind. He had seemed so compassionate, caring, and respectful, but he showed me that he was nothing more than a selfish, evil jerk wanting to take advantage of teenage girls. Wanting to take advantage of them, while their thoughts were swayed with love for him. Today, he had taken off his mask but so had I.

That was the one unwritten law in Imperium. *If you take off your mask, if you stop obscuring yourself with lies, your world will be darker than the night sky. Darker than the black hole that used to be our Sun.* From today on, I would be a new person. I would change my name for the second time in my life but, this time I wouldn't be running away from wanted signs and photos across the media. This time I would be running away from myself.

Nova Osborne.

Courtney Russell

I went over to my closet and pulled out my last shirt. It was white with black polka dots. I walked over to my bed, gently folded the shirt, and placed it on top of the pile emerging from my suitcase. Okay, everything was set. I had taken everything I needed for space. Everything that mattered dearly to me. Everything. No, almost everything.

I paced around the room a couple times before heading back to the bed. I pressed a finger against my wrist to see what time it was-*8:41*. I liked all the new technologies we had nowadays. It was so much more convenient than in my mom's time. We could simply tap our wrist to find a screen projected onto the skin; it provided us with all needed information. According to Luna's further explanations, we would be leaving in three hours or so. Oh gosh, when was Dominik going to pack all his things? He had been at Whitney's for almost two hours.

I looked down at my wrist, annoyed that this person texted me when we're about to evacuate from Earth. I swiped my finger and opened up the text. It was from Dominik.

I'm not coming to the new
planet. I'm staying here.
Read: 8:42 pm

What was he talking about? Was Dominik crazy or was this one of his lame jokes? He would not stay on Earth. I wasn't losing another person to bravery. Staying on Earth would kill him. I tapped the reply button and started typing.

What? No, you're not
staying on Earth.
Tell me what happened.
Read: 8:42 pm

I'm staying.
Read: 8:43 pm

What about Whitney?
Are you just going
to abandon her?
Read: 8:43 pm

Don't talk to
me about her.
Read: 8:43 pm

So it's something
to do with Whitney?
Read: 8:44 pm

I said, don't
talk about her!
Read: 8:44 pm

Okay. But can you just
tell me or are you going
to be the jerk you
always are?
Read: 8:45 pm

Courtney, stop.
I'm not a jerk!
And I can't tell you.
Read: 8:46 pm

I can't help you if
you don't tell
me what's wrong.
Read: 8:46 pm

You wouldn't want
to help me even
If you got the
chance. Admit it,
Courtney, you're as
selfish and bratty as
Luna, mom, AND dad!
Read: 8:48 pm

Don't talk about Luna
like that! If anyone's
a selfish brat, it's you.
Read: 8:49 pm

I'm not a selfish
brat!
Read: 8:49 pm

Of course you are!
You're a rude
maniac as well.
Read: 8:50 pm

I am not! Tell me
one time when I
was mean to you!
Read: 8:51 pm

In second grade,
you put a frog
in my water bottle.
Read: 8:51 pm

That was in second
grade! It doesn't count.
Tell me about a time

I was mean to you
When I became mature.
Read: 8:52 pm

Mature?!!? What are
you talking about?
You still aren't mature!
Read: 8:52 pm

Not funny.
Read: 8:53 pm

Last year, you told my
friends that you saw
me kissing Kyle
on the balcony.
Read: 8:54 pm

Kyle had a girlfriend!
And that girlfriend
happened to be your
best friend, Clarisse!
Read: 8:54 pm

Ugh, just tell
me what's wrong.
Read: 8:55 pm

Whitney turned out
to be Ruby Cox
and Ethan's daughter.
Read: 8:57 pm

No way.
Read: 8:58 pm

Yes, she told me so
herself. It's not
Something to be proud
of. I dumped
her because, well,
she's probably just
like her parents.
How bad will this be
for my reputation?
Read: 9:00 pm

Very bad.
Read: 9:01 pm

I agree.
Read: 9:02 pm

Is this why you
don't want to
evacuate?
Read: 9:02 pm

Yes and no.
Read: 9:03 pm

Explain.
Read: 9:04 pm

She kind of hurt me,
you know. Lying to me
and hiding that just
showed me that she never
trusted me, which is sad,
because I trusted her.
Read: 9:06 pm

And with that our conversation concluded. For once I hoped
Dominik had some sense in him.

Dominik Russell

I walked down Pulchra Street, keeping my eyes on the filthy
streets. I was an idiot to believe that she was from the second class. Who
knows what crimes she's already committed? But why do I think that
she's a criminal? Just because her parents were? I don't know. I am
confused. Anyway, I despise her for lying to me!

I turned left toward Jackson Hall and kept on going until I saw
a beautiful girl with short blonde hair sitting on the curb. Her skinny body
trembled as she sobbed. I slowly ventured closer to her, careful as not to
scare her.

"Excuse me, are you alright?"

"I. . . I'm fine, thank you." she said as she started walking away.

"Can I help you in any way?"

"Yes, you can. Please leave me alone."

"I can't leave you like this, though." I said, concerned. "Please tell
me what has happened."

"I can't do that. I don't even know you."

"Okay. I'm Dominik. What's your name?"

"What don't you understand? Leave me alone!"

"But I can't leave you like this." I pleaded. "Please let me help
you."

"And how could you help me? My mother just died!" screamed the beautiful girl.

"Oh, I'm so sorry. That's so unfortunate." I said, deeply distressed by this fact. "If you need to cry on somebody's shoulder, I'll stick around."

"Don't you have something else to do? And why would you think that I want your help?"

"I don't know. You look pretty heartbroken to me." I said, as I sat down. "I have nothing else to do."

"You're an annoying creep, did you know that?"

"If it makes you feel better to think of me in that way, go ahead." I told her, shrugging.

We kept on walking in silence.

"Thank you for caring." she said.

"No problem."

"My mom had Pollution Cancer and was battling it for many years. But she lost that battle."

"May I ask what your name is?"

"Evelyn. Evelyn Atherton. You might of heard of my mom, Leila Atherton. She was one of the scientists on the NASA research team for technology and cosmological development." she explained, the tears slowly drying. "You know, that was before she was diagnosed with Pollution Cancer. Before the Sun went out."

"What about your dad?"

"Oh, he . . . um . . . we lost him in the Third World War."

"Oh, I'm so sorry." I said. This time I could actually relate to her problems. "Mine, too."

"Oh, that must be terrible." she said. "What's your name?"

"Dominik Russell."

"You're from the Russell family? Oh my god, I've heard so much about you, your mom, your sister, your other sister!"

"Oh yeah, that's nice, I guess."

By now, everyone left in the diner was staring at us. It must be out of the ordinary to see the son of a NASA celebrity trying to comfort a sobbing mess of a girl.

I looked down at my wrist and saw a text message from Courtney. Apparently she'd read the one I sent earlier about not coming to the other planet.

"Uh, excuse me for a moment." I said, as I inched away. What would Courtney want this time? I don't know how long I was in there but after a long text message with Courtney, I knew that for once, she was right. I had to convince Evelyn to come to the other planet with me. I mean, it wouldn't be right just to leave her. The way she looked at me. The way I felt when I was near her, I had never felt that way. I felt amazing. I came walked over to Evelyn

"Oh, Evelyn, I know this is hard on you, but your life will continue on the spaceship with the rest of humanity." I said, quoting Courtney. "You don't have a mom to worry about anymore. Yay, freedom!"

"YOU SELFISH, CRUEL, JERK! HOW CAN YOU SAY THAT JUST BECAUSE I DON'T HAVE PARENTS THAT I GET FREEDOM? HOW? BET YOU'VE NEVER EXPERIENCED SOMETHING LIKE THIS! NOW IF YOU DON'T MIND, GET OUT MY WAY!"

"In fact, I do know. My dad died when I was five. I don't remember a lot of him. My mom thinks it's heroic to stay on Earth and control the spaceship from here. Soon, I'll be an orphan, like you, and there's nothing I can do about it."

"FINE! I DON'T CARE! THAT'S YOUR PROBLEM AND I HAVE MINE! LEAVE ME ALONE!"

I watched her disappear down the street. So much for trying, but it was something. I silently hoped that I would see her again.

I turned down the street that lead to my house and forced my feelings down. I knew that Evelyn's reaction was normal. When your parents die, you are expected to cry, to sob, to hurt. But I wasn't normal. I was numb. I didn't cry, even though I knew my mom was going to die. I needed to pack up. I sighed and started to run, darkness spreading in front of me like a blanket.

Here we go.

Evelyn Atherton

I rushed to Dawson Hospital, uncontrollable tears streaming down my face the whole way. Who did Dominik think he was? I cared for my mother more than I did for anybody. More than I did for myself. I pushed the door open, and got hit by the smell of sterile white floors, walls, and air. Everything was spotlessly clean. I rushed to the receptionist desk.

"Can I see Leila Atherton?" I asked, urgency taking over my voice. The receptionists typed for a moment then, looked at me with a sad expression.

"Are you under 18?" she asked, though her voice was pure monotone, her face was etched with worry lines.

"Yes, I'm under 18."

"How old?"

"16,"

"Okay honey, do you have a legal guardian or some other parent?" she asked. Her black rimmed glasses outlined purple irises and her lips were ruby red. I doubted this was all real. She was probably wearing the *No-show lipstick* and purple contact lenses. But why would she have lenses under glasses? The receptionist looked young, about my older sister Lauren's age. I pushed the thought away and focused on her question.

"No. Leila Atherton was my only living parent." I replied, fighting the tears that sprang to my eyes.

"I'm so sorry to hear that. Do you have older siblings? Perhaps, siblings over the age of 18?" she asked. She didn't seem to care, though, no matter what she said. She seemed to be in a hurry to go home.

"Um, my sister Lauren. She's 19. Lauren Atherton."

"Good. I'll find her mailing address and will send her the bills. For now, fill out this simple paperwork." she said, pushing a clipboard with a packet of paper work. I nodded and found a seat near the elevators and started filling out the questionnaire on the tablet.

First, middle, and last name?

Evelyn Delta Atherton

. . .

I returned tablet to the receptionist. She smiled at me wearily and tapped a button. A receipt printed out and she handed it to me, so I could sign it. Her golden name tag glinted in the light of the lights. *Camila Brooks At Your Service!*

How nice.

Camila motioned for me to follow her, and so I did. Before entering the sterilized hallway with dead bodies, she handed me a mask, some things to slip on over your shoes, and gloves. I felt like a surgeon when I put them on and it did not feel good. She opened the door, scanning her employee ID card and in we went. On our way to wherever we were going, Camila looked at me, sadness in her expression. Though, I couldn't see her very well from the mask, I could tell she felt sorry for me. I didn't want her to, though. Pity was for the weak.

"You know, I was best friends with your sister Lauren, back in my third grade year." she said, sadness now covering her voice like ice on a frozen lake. "Lauren was a nice girl. I liked her. As was your mother. I remember she always used to greet us with cookies."

I recalled how when I was young, my sister did have a best friend coming to the house a lot. Mom would greet them with cookies. The name of my sister's best friend had gotten lost over the years, though.

"I remember you, Evelyn. I remember how you played with Cara, Bella and us. It was like we were one happy family. You were only five, weren't you? I think you were because Bella was three."

I flinched at my sister's names. My twin sister, Cara, was . . . well. . . bratty. You couldn't hang out with her without being criticized to rubbish. She was too good for you, period. She thought our family was so lame, she'd gone to live with her friend Darla Frost. I'd only see her at school and even then, she pretended I didn't exist.

Bella, my younger sister, had stayed with my aunt. World War III had made Miami into a war zone. Bella was young, probably four, maybe five. It hadn't been safe for her. We sent her to live with our Aunt Malena in Iceland. It was peaceful there, at least. My aunt, though, didn't have enough room for Cara, Lauren, and me and we were forced to stay in Miami. I hadn't seen Bella in years. Everything was painful. Life was painful. The only sister that I could talk to and hang out with was Lauren. But, well . . . she was 19. She went to college in California and I missed her dearly.

"Why are you telling me this?" I asked Camila as were neared a door.

"I hoped to bring you some good memories in these dark times, but it obviously didn't work. Your mom is in this room. I'll leave you alone. I'll come to escort you back to the main room in ten minutes time." said Camila, sighing as she opened the door. Then she turned and walked away and I was left staring at my mother's dead body.

Dr. Marcy Brown

"Jacob! Jacob, come down here! Did you see the news?" I yelled as I stepped into the house. A small figure came running down the stairs. My four year old son was soon in front of me. I saw his curly brown hair and his childish face. He still had some baby-ish features. His chubby arms swayed along his side. He was wearing his usual red trousers and his orange shirt.

"Mama!" he yelled, sprinting across the room, and burying his face in my jeans. "You came back! Mama! I'm cold, an' dark!"

"You're cold and dark or outside it's cold and dark?" I asked him, trying to keep my voice light and happy. He didn't need to know my worry.

"Outside, Mama! Outside!" he squealed. I heard footsteps coming down the stairs and looked up. Mackenzie Clark, the babysitter, was coming down the stairs.

"Good evening, Dr. Brown. Now that you're here I'll be going home." she said, putting her shoes on. "I'll see you later, Jacob."

"Mackenzie, what about your payment?" I asked, picking up Jacob and hugging him against my chest. "I've been absent in this house for two weeks. You've been here for two weeks instead of going home. Surely, you want your payment. I've already made the calculations. I pay you ten dollars per hours. That's 240 dollars per day. You were here for sixteen days, so that's 3,840 dollars. Please, Mackenzie, you've done me a huge favor. Let me pay you back."

"Dr. Brown, when are you going to understand that my family is wealthy. I'm not doing *this* because of the money. I'm doing this to *help* you. I won't need the money when we're on the spaceship. I won't. But you, you're a single mother. I know it must be hard for you, so please, keep the money to yoursel-"

"Nonsense! I will pay you back one way or another!" I yelled, but stopped when I felt Jacob flinching away from me. "Oh baby, don't be scared. Mama's not yelling at you."

I heard the front door open and Mackenzie was gone. Foolish child. She'd done so much for me. And for Jacob. I looked down at Jacob's chubby face. He looked so much like his father. So little like me. Who knows, maybe one day his personality would be like mine. Maybe. Or maybe not.

"C'mon, Jacob. We need to pack."

"Up?" he asked, his childish voice ringing in my ears.

"Yes, Jacob. Up."

I looked into his childish face again, now seeing nothing but his father. His awful father. Nowadays, I couldn't look at him without seeing Karl. Without seeing the pain I endured when he left me, six months pregnant. But I also saw a kind, gentle soul. A sweetheart ready to sew the shattered pieces of my heart together. An angel ready to blind me with newfound hope.

When I got upstairs, I put Jacob down on the bed and rushed to my drawer, hastily pulling out clothes and stuffing them into the first suitcase I had found.

"Mama, wha happening?" asked Jacob, tilting his head sideways like a confused dog. "Are we going *zoom, zoom*?"

"Yes, Jacob." I muttered, as I threw a blouse into the suitcase. "We're going *zoom, zoom. Zoom, zoom* to outer space." I said, trying to sound cheerful for Jacob's sake.

"Reawy?" he asked, his voice full of amazement, his eyes full of wonder. "Ouer space?"

"Yes, now will you bring all your clothes from your room?"

"Yes, Mama." he said, as he slid off the bed and skipped toward his room.

I sighed.

He was so happy. I was blessed to have him.

I heard steps and seconds later, Jacob came into the room with a bundle of clothes.

"Mama, Jacob back!" he yelled, speeding into the room with a bundle of clothes.

"Jacob, will that be enough clothes?" I asked him. By my calculations, we'd be in space for about three years. I wanted him to have enough clothes. We'd be boarding the Urania 2.7 and then the small Miami ship would connect into the grand Super Astra. All cities would have a separate Urania ship to board. I wondered if China had made the Super Astra big enough for the 50 billion people on Earth. I hoped they had. I couldn't stand leaving more people behind. I didn't want to admit it, but Audrey was right. The prisoners would just cause havoc if we let them board one of the Urania's.

My gaze fell back onto the pile of clothes that Jacob had brought me. Super Astra was supposed to have pools, spas, malls, banks, playgrounds, and other things, but who knew if they would supply humans with children's clothes. I sighed and threw Jacob's clothes into the almost full suitcase. There was just enough room for a couple other things I wanted to take with me. I walked over to the drawer and pulled out the picture of Karl and me. I remembered that day clearly. Too clearly. As if it was yesterday.

We had gone to the park, and we were having a great time. He pushed me on the swings, his dazzling smile filling me up with emotions I couldn't comprehend. I had laughed hard and had had a great time. His chocolate brown eyes shined with happiness. We had asked a tourist to take the picture for us and later put that picture on the drawer in our room. I had just found out that I was expecting a baby. We were both so delighted and happy. Words couldn't describe it well enough. But something had changed. Karl never told me the reason but he abandoned Jacob and me.

I snapped out of my shock and put the picture back on the drawer. Super Astra would help me start from a new chapter. A blank page. That picture would only bring back painful memories from the past. I zipped up the suitcase and picked up Jacob, hugging him close to me, as if he might disappear in a puff of smoke.

"Mama, wha abou Shaggy?" asked Jacob.

Right. Shaggy was his imaginary friend that Jacob could never leave.

"Where's Shaggy?" I asked, fake curiosity in my voice. Gosh, it even sounded fake to me. I put Jacob down and told him, "Go find Shaggy. Quickly. Go, go, go!"

Jacob ran out of the room and turned the corner. I grabbed the suitcase and dragged it behind me, the suitcase creating more and more noise with every stair it hit. Thump. Thump! THUMP! I gently put down the suitcase and started up the stairs once more, but Jacob was quicker than me.

"Found him!" he yelled, while pulling an imaginary arm down the stairs.

"Great! Now we'll just put him into the suitcase. Shaggy won't mind that, right?"

Jacob didn't say anything. I opened the suitcase and Jacob put an imaginary body into it. I zipped up the suitcase and picked up Jacob, again.

"Do you want to take anything else?"

"No, Mama."

I picked up the suitcase and dragged it behind me out of the door. This was the last I would see of my home, my city, my planet.

We walked to the NASA space center of Miami and I left my suitcase with Madison, the luggage clerk. I saw her worried expression, and tried to give her a comforting smile but I probably looked like I was getting strangled. Madison though, didn't return it. I watched our suitcase go down the conveyor belt and disappear through the black rubber flaps.

"Let's go, Jacob. We'll be boarding soon." I said, as I walked down the sterile hallways. Every surface gleamed like a mini-sun. The windows were large and clearly displayed the night sky. The stars glittered as the Milky Way sat by them. It looked like a jeweled necklace on somebody's collar bone. Jacob hugged me and pulled himself closer. I regained myself as I heard the sound of a vacuum cleaner come closer and closer. Right. Jacob was scared of loud noises.

"It's okay, baby. It's not going to hurt you." I whispered into his ear. He stared up at me with those endless brown eyes as if I had said something insane. As if I had sprouted a third eye.

"Mama, it's woud!" he complained, tearing up.

"Baby, Mama's with you." I said, gently stroking his hair with my free arm. "There's nothing to be afraid of. Mama will protect you. You're safe."

I steered us in the opposite direction. I knew it would take longer to get to the deport rails, but we would still get there. I had the map of the NASA building memorized in my head from years of working here. I hoped we wouldn't run into any loud noises because there was no other way of getting to the deport rails. Gently placing my hand on his back, I started to hum a lullaby from my childhood.

Luna Russell

"Tickets! NASA families to the left! Other people to the right! Move it, move it, move it! We don't have much time! Three suitcases per family! That is the maximum! No exceptions! NASA families are allowed five suitcases per family!" yelled a woman who's name tag glinted *Rebekah Daniels*. She had blue hair that looked so ridiculous, it would've made me laugh out loud if it weren't for the look on her face. She wore a sharp looking business suit. It was black with no hint of color. It was boring with no sense of creativity whatsoever. Could business suits have creativity? Probably not.

I looked around, relieved to see that my siblings hadn't run off. Courtney was on my left and Dominik on my right. We had packed his luggage for him, since he came home really late. Both Courtney and Dominik were showing no expression, no feeling on their faces. They were blank as an unfinished mask. I hugged Cassie closer to my chest.

"What're your names?" yelled the screeching woman. It took me a moment to realize that she was yelling at us. I turned to answer he question but Dominik was quicker.

"Dominik Alyx Russell and Courtney Ciare Russell." he said, pride obscuring his voice. Then he looked at me and smirked as if I was worth nothing more than a penny. "Oh, and Luna Selene Russell."

"In what department does Audrey Russell work in?" she yelled. I felt like in the middle of a quiz. This time, I was quicker than Dominik.

"Aerospace Engineering," I answered, my voice as clear as a bell. Dominik looked at me as if I had taken away his money and bought something with it. His gaze was murderous, but I ignored it, focusing my attention on Rebekah Daniels.

"Before Rolf Russell passed away, what department did he work in when he was at NASA?"

"Meteorology," I answered. Now Courtney was watching me with disgust.

"You truly are the children of Audrey and Rolf Russell." she said, now expressing so much fake kindness, I wanted to barf. "Your mother made a great sacrifice. A sacrifice Imperium will remember for a long time. You may proceed through this gate. If you turn left, down the first corridor, you will find your private chambers. You will later receive instructions on where to go to get to your private chambers aboard the Super Astra. Thank you for choosing to fly with Urania 2.7!" said Rebekah Daniels. She opened a gate behind her and ushered us in. Once we were out of earshot Dominik began muttering.

"What else did we have to choose? The next Urania is stationed all the way in Jacksonville."

"Shut it, Dominik!" retorted Courtney. We turned down the hallway and soon found a door labeled, *Russell Family*. "Well, I guess this is it."

"If you have to guess, your stupidity is more than your wanna-be beauty," replied Dominik, a smug smile on his lips.

"How are we supposed to open it?" asked Courtney, flipping her hair behind her back. "We have no key."

"Stupid beauty," muttered Dominik as he turned the doorknob. It turned with no resistance. The door opened wide but stopped before hitting the wall. An automatic door. I should've guessed.

"What did you just say?" snapped Courtney.

"Stupid beauty," said Dominik in a most casual way. "You know, instead of sleeping beauty."

Courtney growled at Dominik but stopped when we saw our room. Before us spread a large living room. It contained a couch, and automatic armchair, a T.V., and a couple of astronomical paintings. The walls were painted grey and the floor was made of robot-made tiles. The tiles were all hand-painted by robots and you could tell because each had incredible details that the present day human wouldn't be able to make. No human being could have made such precise artwork as the one on the tiles. Each tile was unique as each and every one displayed a different scene. One showed a NASA scientist peering through a telescope. Another showed Neil Armstrong- the first person to walk on the moon, walking on the moon. Another displayed our Solar System with no Sun and another displayed the Milky Way.

To my left was a door, that I guessed would lead to the bathroom. A door to my right was open. It was a plain closet. Nothing really interesting. A door stood at the end of the living room and we quickly made our way to see what hid behind it. When we opened it there were four doors. We all went through all of them and it turned out to be three different bedrooms, all the same size. The last door turned out to be a small kitchenette with a table and four chairs.

Courtney and Dominik each claimed their rooms leaving me with the room nearest to the kitchenette.

I opened the door and stepped inside. Before me spread a large lightroom. The walls were painted white and the carpet resembled the Andromeda Galaxy. It was breathtakingly beautiful. There were no windows, as I expected. To my right was a closet with mirrored doors. In front of me lay a bed with plain sheets. I walked forward and found a desk to my left. It was crammed with astronomical objects such as small telescopes, Armillary spheres, small imitations of planets, sextants, orreries, and more. The desk itself was also white but there were blue Christmas lights outlining the whole thing. I took one more step forward and let Cassie go. The room was amazing, just like my dream room. I walked toward the bed and saw that my luggage had been transported and was sitting on the floor waiting for me. I sighed, jumped over them, and flung myself onto the bed. It was just right. Not too hard but not too soft. Just right.

"Welcome aboard the Urania 2.7!" beamed a voice from invisible speakers. The sound startled me and I jumped. Cassie, on the other hand was unaffected. She had found herself a cat bed under the desk and was now dozing off. "I hope you have everything you need for the moment. My name is Venus and I'm one of the helpful crew you will encounter on the Urania 2.7! Please stay silent and patient while I review the safety and emergency routes."

I went silent with the rest of the ship. Just like Venus had told us to.

"If we run out of fuel before we get to the Super Astra, we must depart in emergency ships. Simply go down to the docks and fly a ship. It's already programmed to automatically lead you to the Super Astra. Six hundred people per ship, please. Also, please refrain from smoking and/or drinking in prohibited areas. There will be special rooms set for smoking and separate rooms for drinking." said Venus, temporarily pausing to catch her breath. "In order to guarantee you a safe passage through the Urania 2.7 you will have to refrain from using employee passageways. Please only walk through the corridors marked with blue light. I will now hand you over to my colleague, Noelle."

I heard the speaker being moved and then a new voice projected across the ship.

"Hello there, passengers of Urania 2.7! This is Noelle Si-- oh what? But Ms. Christabelle Carey told me I could say my last name. What? I can't? Okay." said Noelle, her voice now unsure and shaking. "We have seven emergency exits on this ship. Two in the front, two in the back, two in the middle of the ship, and one from the roof. In order to open all of them, you must pull the red handle toward you and then turn it to your left. Information centers are located in every accessible hallway for your convenience. My colleague Oceane will explain to you all the features on this ship that have been added for your convenience."

Unlike Venus, before her, Noelle had a high-pitched, squeaky voice. She could've played a mouse on Broadway and she would've played it perfectly.

"Now that all of our expected passengers have boarded the Urania 2.7, I will be introducing all the features on this ship. If you go through hallway 57, you'll be able to enjoy the complimentary spa. Of course, it's complimentary if you're one of the star families, which include the Brown family, the Russell family, the Rune family, the Smith family, the Sparks family, the King family, the Doyle family, and the Zimmerman family. If you're from another NASA family, which means if your grandma or grandpa has worked at NASA, you can enjoy all the features of this ship with a minimum payment. All others to enjoy these features must pay full price. On floor 67, you'll-"

"--be able to enjoy the pools, jacuzzis, saunas, and steam rooms. No robots are allowed in these areas. On floor 31--"

But I no longer listened. I was bored. I needed to get out of this . . . place.

I jumped off the bed and opened the door, leaving it open behind me. I sped through the hallway, the lights casting shadows on the wall as I moved.

"Courtney, I'm going out to explore the ship." I yelled, not waiting for an answer before I opened the door and stepped into the hallway. I turned left and soon found myself by one of the pools that Oceane had mentioned. It was an Olympic sized pool with four large, diamond-shaped jacuzzis next to it. On my left was an information center. Another thing the ladies had mentioned. I sped toward it and soon found myself searching for a peaceful place. The library. It was perfect.

According to the map, it was only a couple floors up. My eyes darted across the map, searching for the elevator nearest to me. There. It was behind me. I spun around and sure enough, an elevator with gleaming doors sat behind me. I darted across the room and pressed the *UP* button. I was on floor 14. The library was on floor 19. The ladies were still speaking in the invisible speakers hanging overhead but I paid them no attention. As soon as the elevator doors opened I stepped forward ready to speed right in but an unexpected figure knocked me down on the black carpet. Pain sprang up in my left arm and tears flooded my eyes. I tried to move, but every move was painful and too hard.

"I'm so sorry, Miss." said a voice. A boy. "Are you hurt? Can you get up?" The person flipped me onto my back and I got my first good glance at the boy. He was my age or something like that. His hair was wild and blond, sticking up and out from all sorts of directions. He had cobalt blue eyes, unlike my ice blue eyes, which looked like tiny galaxies. He wore a black sweatshirt with a snarling tiger on the front of it. He finished the look off with khaki colored jeans and blacksneakers.

"Are you okay, Miss?" he asked, now frantic. "Do you need help?" I tried to stand up using my right hand and surprisingly, it worked.

"Please don't call me *Miss*," I said, closing my eyes and willing the pain in my left hand to subside.

"What's your name, then?" he asked, relief dawning over his face once he saw me get up.

"Luna Russell," I breathed.

"You're Luna Russell?" he asked, his eyes widening. "Are you from the Star family?"

I couldn't manage an answer. I just nodded.

"Wow." I glared at him and he quickly schooled his expression. "I mean, I'm sorry. I'm Oscar Smith."

"Star Smith family?" I asked, raising one eyebrow.

"Uh-huh. You don't look too good. I'll take you to the doctor."

"There's a doctor on this ship?" I asked, trying to think of something the ship didn't have. If the Urania 2.7 had this many things, what about the Super Astra?

Oscar laughed, his voice sounding very pleasant. Wait, what? What was I thinking about? His eyes, his perfection. *Stop it!*, I said, silently scolding myself.

"Yes, there's a doctor on this ship."

"Hmm, would it be safe to walk through the corridors while the ship is taking off?"

"You'll be fine."

We walked on some more, but I couldn't keep track of time. Everytime I tried to move something, a finger or my wrist, pain would shoot back and blind me. After what seemed like hours, Oscar finally announced, "We're here."

I opened my eyes.

Sure enough, we were in a medical room, and from what I could see, medical supplies and machines were scattered everywhere. The room itself was white with cold white tiles beneath me. It smelled of chemicals and every surface gleamed as if to show off that it was clean.

"What can I do for you today?" asked a robotic voice. I looked up to see a robot but not just any robot, a medical robot. It had pale skin and wires jutting out from it's head. I highly doubted that was the initial design. It wore a purple surgery gown and blue slippers.

"Please call the doctor."

The robot turned and left the room, leaving us alone. The machines nearest to us buzzed and hummed creating a weirdly comforting mood.

"Where were you trying to get to?" asked Oscar as he inspected my hand with his eyes. "You were in quite a hurry."

"The library," I answered, once again trying to move one of my fingers but yelping out with pain. "I needed some peace and quiet. Sorry I crashed into you."

"It's okay. Things like this happen, you know." said Oscar, as he casually sat in a spinning chair. I was quite sure that it was meant for the doctor. "Who are you on the ship with?"

"My siblings," I answered in a monotone voice.

"No mom?"

"Nope. She decided to be heroic and stayed on Earth, to control the Urania." After finishing this sentence, I started to slightly tear up, but before a tear could roll down my cheek, I blinked it back.

"Oh. Sorry about that. What about your dad?"

"World War Three,"

"Oh. I'm very sorry to hear that," said Oscar, now leaning forward. "You seem to take it in. . . good."

"My dad died when I was about one. I was never really close to my mom," I answered, trying to keep my eyes from going to his eyes. "Who are you here with?"

"My mom, my dad, and my younger and older siblings."

"How old are they?"

"Well, Alexander just turned seventeen and Gabrielle is ten." said Oscar, now spinning around like a little kid. "What about your siblings?"

"They're both sixteen."

"Tough."

"Agreed."

There was a moment of awkward silence between us in which, we both stared at each other. Luckily, the doctor came in.

"We haven't even flown off and you come in here hurt!" exclaimed the doctor. She faced me and I got a good view of her. She was a middle aged woman, or so it seemed. It was hard to tell because she wore a mask, gloves, and had very short brown hair. She wore a white coat over blue sweatpants. Interesting choice. The doctor, at least from what I could see, had hazel eyes. I sat on the blue bed by the corner and pretended that the arm didn't hurt that much. "What happened?"

"I. . . I'm not sure." said Oscar, eyeing my arm in a ridiculous manner. "She. . . I crashed into her by accident and. . . her arm hurts."

"I see." said the doctor. She turned to me and came closer to inspect my arm. "Honey, let me see that arm."

I stretched the hand toward her and she gently took it. She inspected the hand, turning it over and gently pressing points. I yelped when it hurt and dried the tears that sprang to my eyes when it didn't hurt.

"It's badly sprained." said the doctor. "What's your name, honey?"

The doctor turned her chair and situated herself in front of a computer. She typed some things; the password I guessed. Then, she looked at me expectantly.

"Luna. Selene. Russell." I said, sneaking a glance over at Oscar. He looked worried, but there was also a tinge of amusement on his face. Why was he so unreadable?

"Luna Selene Russell. Is that right?" asked the doctor.

"Y—yes," I stammered.

I didn't know why I was nervous. Almost everything required all three of your names these days. But that thought didn't make my worries subside. Really? Really? Of all the times that I was usually calm, I had to be nervous now? What was I nervous about, anyway? I sneaked a glance at Oscar, and my heart sped up. It started beating like a frantic bird trying to escape its cage. That was it. Oscar.

"So he crashed into you?" asked the doctor as she eyed Oscar.

"N-no, no. I was hurrying to get to the library and I crashed into him." I explained.

"Hmm, well that's peculiar," said the doctor as she pushed away from the desk. "The *guy* told me that he crashed into you."

"The *guy's* name is Oscar." said Oscar, leaning casually on the wall. His hands were crossed and. . . he looked like a god. Not joking. He was so intimidatingly. . . perfect. "And that's not right. I think she hit her head as she fell. I think. I crashed into her. Her memory must be hazy or something."

I glared at Oscar. What was he doing?

"I see. Well, I'll check your head." said the doctor as she turned back toward me.

"What about her arm?" asked Oscar.

"I believe that she badly sprained her wrist." explained the doctor.

"Ouch." said Oscar, as he grimaced. "How long will it take to heal?"

"About two weeks." said the doctor as she sped toward a closet I hadn't noticed before. "I'll give you a wrist brace." she said, now turning back to me. "You can take pain medicine if the pain is too much to handle. Please check in with me again after the two weeks. If you have any other concerns or if you're showing concerning symptoms please do find me before your next scheduled appointment. My name is Dr. Cheryl Nelson."

Dr. Cheryl Nelson walked to me and gently put the brace on. Once she secured the Velcro she patted me on the head. I gave her an unapproving look.

"Great! You can now check out with the front office and book your appointment." said the doctor as she sat in her chair and shifted her gaze to the computer. I looked at Oscar to see what he was doing. But why did I want to do this?

Oscar shrugged and walked toward me.

"Let's go," he said, as he tugged my good hand. I stood up, but crumbled back on the bed, but nausea overwhelmed me. The room was spinning. Round and around and around and around. "Whoa Luna! Careful! You're going to hurt your other arm!" hissed Oscar, as he tried to pull me up. "Okay, we can do this slowly."

Oscar pulled me up at an extremely slow pace, just as he'd promised. This time the nausea didn't come.

"Right then. How are you feeling?" Oscar asked me.

"Great," I muttered, sarcasm clouding over my answer.

"That's amazing to hear. Let's go check you out."

Oscar walked me down an endless hallway. At least that's what it felt like. We walked and we walked and we walked until we reached a door labeled: *Check out, payments, and next appointments.* Oscar pushed the door open and a cool breeze hit my face. It was refreshing, to one extent.

We walked over to a check-out desk. The guy looked more like a rebel from a gang rather than a man working in a hospital. But hey, everyone is weird in their own way. Oscar cleared his throat and the man finally looked up at us.

"Oh hello, what can I do for you today?" asked Obsidian with a normal voice. Not too deep but not too high and squeaky. "I wasn't expecting patients 'till we took off. Nausea usually hits then. So what can I do for you today?"

"We need to make an appointment." said Oscar, cutting the receptionist off. He wrapped a protective hand around my shoulders, pulling me toward him. I looked up at him. My skin tingled where he touched me. What was he doing? I looked at the receptionist to see his greedy eyes scanning my body. He was dangerous, I could tell. And danger was not good.

"May I have the patient's name, please?" asked the receptionist, once again, scanning me. For the first time, I felt grateful that I was here with Oscar. Oscar looked at me, and I realized I had to speak.

"Luna Selene Russell." I said, clearing my throat. What was wrong with me? I would be out of here in no time. I shouldn't fear this. . . person.

"Spell that."

"L-U-N-A S-E-L-E-N-E R-U-S-S-E-L-L," I said with confidence, lifting my chin up higher. Slightly. Just slightly.

I said all the needed information and soon we were free to go. Oscar walked me away from the hospital.

"Where do you want to go?" he asked me, now letting go of me. My skin abruptly stopped tingling with warmth. I looked up at him, studying his features carefully. What was there to do?

"Attention all passengers. We will now take off. Please lean near a wall, and hold on tight to the nearest, most sturdy object you can find. I repeat, we will now take off." said one of the girls from before, her voice blaring through invisible speakers.

I heard the hum of the engine start. I didn't even have to tell Oscar, we walked to the nearest wall in unison. It smelled of fresh paint. It was amazing. I stood by the wall but there was no object in sight. Except maybe for the T.V. hanging above our heads. I would probably break it, though. I slid to the floor, the cool tiles cooling my entire body. Oscar copied me. The steady hum of the engine grew louder, and soon we were holding onto each other to keep from toppling over. But the commotion didn't last long. It was obvious when the spaceship lifted from the ground. Almost too obvious. I sat back down, criss-cross, my hands in my lap.

I sat there, just looking at the other wall, parallel from us. I was leaving everything behind. My school, my house, my dad's grave, my. . . mom. I hadn't noticed the silent, uncontrollable tears streaming down my face, until Oscar gently wiped them.

"What are you thinking about?" he asked.

"I. . . I admire your freedom. It's like you have no boundaries."

"Well, I mean everyone has boundaries, but I have less." he said, grinning from ear to ear. That smile. It made my heart stop beating for a few seconds. "But forget about me. What's happening?"

"My mom. She decided to stay and give coordinates to the ship or whatever." I explained, now the tears were flowing freely. "She's on Earth, when I'm up here. And I couldn't do anything about it."

"Oh well. . ."

Even Oscar seemed lost for words. After a long time of just sitting there on the cold, hostile tile, I overcame my shock.

"Where were you going before I crashed into you?"

"My chambers," said Oscar. "But I was only going to get ready for the departure. We can go to the library, if you want."

"No. I was only going there to escape the horrible reality of leaving Earth. I hoped that if I got interested in a good book, I wouldn't get pulled under by reality," I said, trying to keep my voice stable. "I thought. . . I could escape."

"Oh, I'm really sorry to hear that." mumbled Oscar, as he energetically stood up. "We should hang out. You're fun to be around. I could introduce you to my siblings."

"Okay, sure." I said, as I stood up. "You probably don't want to meet mine, though."

"Why not?"

"They're brats,"

"Oh well, that's okay." said Oscar, grinning his hundred-dollar smile. "I think I could handle it."

"If you say so. Courtney might be on a date, and Dominik's probably at a buffet or something."

"Interestingly enough, there's no buffet on the Urania 2.7." said Oscar, pulling me down the hallway by my good arm.

"Oh well, if that's the case, he's probably found his own date." I said, smiling as I caught up. In that moment, I realized that everyone makes their own choices, good or bad, wise or dumb, healthy or unhealthy as they may be, the person who made them suffers the consequences. I decided to make the choice of staying around Oscar and his positive mentality.

Oscar Smith

We walked down the endless hallways of the Urania 2.7. They seemed to go on and on and on, forever and ever and ever. But time, at least for me, was not wasted. Luna was. . . well cute. Her not-brown, not-blond, not-dirty blond hair hung over her shoulders like overcast clouds in a grey sky. Her ice-blue eyes pierced me every time she looked at me. But I would heal when she'd smile at me. It hurt me when she told me that her mom had chosen to be left behind. It hurt me to see her hurt and crying. It made me feel warm and fuzzy on the inside when she was smiling and laughing, which wasn't much given that she had an emotional breakdown and a severely sprained wrist. And I had just met her. And I already felt so. . . complete.

As we walked down the endless hallways, we talked about life, siblings, dreams, and whatnot. She told me her dreams of becoming a NASA research scientist and her obsession over cosmology and astronomy. She told me about her siblings, Courtney and Dominik, and then asked about my life and dreams.

That was hard. Sure, Luna was easy to talk to and she was the exact opposite of what I had heard about her, but talking to anyone about my dreams was. . . well, near impossible. She would surely laugh at me. Her careless, free laugh. Only, I knew it wasn't near careless. From what she'd told me, she'd acted like a "replacement mom" to her older siblings. She had her own problems to deal with. Just like I had my problems. I looked at Luna once more. She had no mask. No lies obscured her actual self. At least, none that I could see. She wore no makeup to fix her outer looks. Not like they needed fixing. She didn't lie to me about anything. I was good at telling when people were lying to me. Their eyes would widen up, they would say over exaggerated things, and they would smile. Finding out why they were lying to you was the hard part. Everyone had masks that had to be penetrated in order to see the truth. Everyone except Luna.

She was cute, but I liked her as a friend.

We passed a couple corridors and then got into the elevator where I had hit her. Where she hit me. Whatever. We talked and talked and talked.

"C'mon, tell me what you dream of," pleaded Luna, her ice-blue eyes once again piercing me. It was hard to resist such temptation.

"Nah, my dreams aren't nearly as interesting as yours. My stories aren't nearly as full of action as yours are," I chided, now leading Luna through another maze of endless corridors that opened before us as the elevator doors opened.

"You can't say that." said Luna, as she bumped her shoulder into mine. The touch sent tingles down my spine. "I've didn't hear any of your stories or dreams or whatever. I don't know if they're interesting or boring."

"Believe me, they're boring."

"I'll believe it when I hear it."

"You're clever, but no." I said, as we turned down yet another corridor. Soon, we were going to get to my chambers. The star family Smith's chambers.

I found myself in front of the door of the Smith family chambers. I reached for the doorknob, turning the cold, hostile brass and opened the door.

"Here we are," I announced.

Luna moved in beside me.

"Wow, it looks exactly like our chambers." she said. I couldn't tell if she was impressed or not.

"I guess the creator of the Urania had no imagination whatsoever."

"Yep," muttered Luna as she went in.

I spotted a figure hiding behind the couch. A flurry of butterscotch blond hair. Everything went by so fast. The figure jumped out the couch, scaring Luna in the process. She screamed and collapsed on the floor near my feet. I was startled but nothing to make me jump.

"Wow! Who's this?" yelled my ten-year old sister Gabrielle. She was dancing in the same clothes she'd last worn. Grey leggings, green sweater, yellow socks, and hot pink slippers. Even I could tell that she had an awful taste in clothes.

"Gabrielle, what were you thinking?" I yelled, crouching near Luna, who was still trembling. "You won't get to know who she is if you give her a heart attack!"

"Heart attack? Yeah, sure." scoffed Gabrielle, spinning around like a mini-tornado. "Is she your girlfriend?"

I considered the question for a moment. If I said yes, then Gabrielle would stop asking questions. But then Luna would think I'm a guy so desperate for love. No, that wasn't an option.

"No, Gabrielle, she's not my girlfriend."

"She's like Vanessa?"

"Who's Vanessa?" asked Luna, still quivering beside me.

"His girlfriend!" beamed Gabrielle.

"You have a girlfriend?" asked Luna, her eyes widening with shock. "She'll think you're cheating on her."

"I do not have a girlfriend," I said, trying to keep myself from exploding. "Vanessa was not my girlfriend. She was a study partner."

"A study partner?" asked Luna, now slowly getting up with the help of the wall. "What school did you go to?"

"Centaurus Academy." I muttered, now embarrassed to have had a study partner. I didn't want Luna getting the wrong impression.

"Centaurus Academy?" beamed Luna, forgetting about the Vanessa-thing. Or so it seemed. "Wow, I've always wanted to go there."

"Didn't you go there? Most Star family's kids went there."

"No, my parents weren't big on investing in education." mumbled Luna, as she leaned against the wall. "I went to Wood's High School. You know, the community high school. The public high school."

"Yeah, I know." I said, as I tried to stifle my surprise. A public high school? Wood's High School? Augh, having wealthy parents pampered me too much. It's okay, though. The school you attend doesn't make you, *you.*

"So is she like Vanessa?"

"No, she's not a study partner. There's nothing to study for."

"A girlfriend?" asked Gabrielle.

"A girlfriend?" asked a deeper voice. "Oscarbob has a girlfriend? I'm surprised."

My brother's figure emerged. I didn't know if he'd been eavesdropping, he was too good of a liar. His platinum blond hair blinded me in the light that the lightbulbs gave off. It was almost white. Almost. His deep gray eyes pierced me but not in a good way. Luna's eyes pierced me in a good way, if there's such thing. Alexander's eyes made me feel small, weak, and insignificant. He wore a blue t-shirt with a golden star shooting across the shirt. Below it the words, *Centaurus Academy- Learn Everything From A To Z!* were written. He wore denim jeans and no socks or shoes. Somehow he rocked that look. He made all the girls squeal when he passed by. To them, he was an angel. I knew better. He was a nightmare dressed as a daydream. The devil dressed as an angel. A bomb in a pretty package. I heard Luna catch her breath and wondered if she saw what most girls saw when Alexander passed by.

"My baby brother has a girlfriend?" asked Alexander, as he stepped closer to Luna. Tipping her chin up with a finger he said, "She's not bad looking, either. A Russell."

"I don't know who you are but don't touch me." growled Luna.

"Haven't you told her about the rest of the family, Oscarbob?"

"Don't call me Oscarbob." I growled, putting myself between Luna and Alexander. "And I did tell her, it's just you're so bad-looking that she couldn't tell you were my bratty seventeen year old brother. You know, I'm so good looking and all."

"You're nothing compared to me. And you'll never be anything more than a scrummy podship pilot," sneered Alexander. Gabrielle danced behind him, making funny faces at all of us. She was enjoying this argument, I could tell. "Tell me, sugarpea, how old are you?"

Alexander pushed me out of the way, so he could talk to Luna. I was sent sprawling on the floor.

"Why do you care?" she answered.

"She's got an attitude," he chided. "Now tell me, *Russell*, what brings you here?"

"Why do you care, *Smith*?"

"Oh, this is getting too good!" squealed Gabrielle.

"These are my chambers, sugarpea. And if you don't answer me quickly then I'm afraid I'll have to take you out of the chambers *my own way*." said Alexander, as he prowled around Luna like a puma waiting for it's prey to die. In the meantime, I stood up. "Say the right thing."

"And according to you, what's the right thing to say?" asked Luna, hiding her wounded hand behind her back.

"Guess." he murmured.

"I'm Oscar's girlfriend. I'm a science nerd, and I'm nothing you would be interested in." responded Luna, in a confident voice.

"You are?" squealed Gabrielle as she attempted a cartwheel only to land with a *thud* on the floor.

"That's great to hear, Oscarbob." said Alexander as he pushed me into the wall again. This time I landed face-first on the floor. Warm, sticky liquid splattered all over my face.

"Okay, I gotta go meet my buddy Viktor." said Alexander as he walked away, stepping on me in the process. "See 'y'all!"

"Oh my gosh! Oh, what's your name?" asked Gabrielle.

"Luna."

"Oh my gosh! Luna, I need to tell you so many things about Oscar!" squealed Gabrielle, as I heard her footsteps getting farther and farther away from me. "Come now! Oscar will be fine."

"I. . . I don't think so."

I felt someone turn me over onto my back and gasp. Luna, probably. Gabrielle didn't give a crap about me.

"Oh Oscar!" gasped Luna, before she stood up and frantically asked Gabrielle, "Where are the tissues?"

"There're some in the bathroom."

I heard Luna's frantic steps as she darted passed me. Sparks and stars sprawled through my vision. Everything was blurry. Alexander didn't usually hit me so hard. Actually, this was the first time he had hit me. What was he trying to prove? That he was stronger than me? Obviously. That he was better than me? Maybe.

Luna came back with a handful of tissues in her hands. She dabbed my face gently and then lifted my head onto her thigh. I recognized the fact that I couldn't feel blood on my face. She probably dried everything up and was elevating my head to stop the blood flow.

"Oscar, I--"

"You're fine, I'm fine, we're all fine." I murmed. "Did he hurt you? Did Alexander hurt you?"

"No," she whispered. "We need to get you to a doctor."

"We can't."

"Why? You need it." asked Luna, panic now evidently rising in her voice. "I know nothing of medicine. I can't cure you."

"The hospital will send a notification to my mom." I explained, now prying my eyes open. My eyesight wasn't blurry anymore. I could see. She was right above me, her face etched with worry lines. "My mom will freak out."

A single tear escaped Luna's left eye. Was it something I said? Oh right, *her* mom wasn't here.

"I know someone who can help." I said, now trying to get up. Surprisingly, I didn't fall down. "Gabrielle, call the Athertons!"

"No, you call them!"

"Gabrielle, please!"

"Fine."

I couldn't hear much of the conversation, since I was in another room. Luna paced after me. I think she was afraid I would collapse any minute, now. No need for worry. I got this. During the agonizing silence, Luna didn't ask who I wanted Gabrielle to call. She didn't show any indication that she was curious. Minutes passed and Gabrielle hadn't told us anything, so I was startled by a knock at the door.

"I'll get it." I said, rushing to the door. The movement made me lightheaded but I refused to let it show. Luna had enough to worry about. So did I.

I opened the door to see Evelyn Atherton. I was expecting Bella. Or Lauren. Maybe their mom, Leila. But not their dad. He'd died in the Third World War. I looked at Evelyn again. I'd last seen her more than half a year ago, and she'd changed quite a bit. Her blonde hair was now short. So short that it hung above her shoulders like overcast clouds over a town. This contrasted a lot with the knee-length hair she used to have. I think short hair looked better on her. It bounced against the sides of her face every time she moved. She still had those soft blue eyes, though. I wasn't sure what I was expecting. Maybe colored contact lenses?

Heavy black mascara outlined her eyes. She wore a black dress with black tights and black high heels. Out of all the colors, why did she choose to dress herself in black? She definitely did not look good in black.

"Oh, hi Evelyn." I said, in my usual loud voice. "What's with the black?"

I noticed a figure sliding up next to me. Startled, I realized it was Luna. For seconds, I had forgotten about her. I glanced back at Evelyn. Her eyes narrowed and she snarled in disgust.

"Who's she, Oscar?"

"Oh, um, this is Luna Russell."

Evelyn once again, snarled with disgust.

"Tell me, Oscar, why did you want me here?"

"Oh actually, I was expecting Bella, but now that you're here I would mind more ladies company."

"And why were you expecting Bella?" asked Evelyn. Her voice was full of poison, as she pretended to be curious. "Did you want her to clean up that bloody mess of a face you have? Because your little girlfriend here, is too fragile to take care of it?"

I glanced over at Luna. She seemed perfectly at ease. Like this didn't make her uncomfortable.

"Look Evelyn, I'm not sure even *you* can clean up this beautiful face."

Evelyn snarled.

"Evelyn, can you just tell me where Bella is?" I asked, throwing in one of my signature smiles to try to convince her to help me. "You know Bella's best at the medical stuff. If you would just tell me, I can let you be in that bad mood of yours."

"Bella went to live in Iceland. I suppose your little excuse for a brain couldn't remember that." she said, as she glared at Luna. "I'm going to meet her in the Super Astra. After all, she's coming in with the Terra 1.4 spaceship."

Right. Each continent had a different series of spaceships.

North America had the Urania spaceships.

South America had the Pluto spaceships.

Africa had the Mars spaceships.

Australia, Oceania, and the other islands had the Andromeda spaceships.

Asia had the Neptunia spaceships.

And Europe had the Terra spaceships.

Although the world had become one big country, the continents and their names still remained.

"Oh."

"Oh's right."

"Evelyn, why are you in such a bad mood?" I asked. "And what's with all the black?"

"It's none of your business, Oscar." she sneered. If her voice was full of hatred and poison, then it was nothing to what came out now.

"Where's Aunt Leila?"

"She's wasn't your aunt." sneered Evelyn. I didn't know who she was. This was not the cheery, bouncy person I knew. Used to know. "Stop playing your childish games, Oscar."

"Okay, then." I started to sprout a fear for Evelyn. What was wrong? "Where's your mother?"

"She's dead." whispered Evelyn as she turned fled down an endless corridor. I didn't bother to go after her. I was too stunned.

Luna Russell

"That's unfortunate." I muttered, as I stared into the now-empty space in front of me. This Evelyn had run off. She was probably mourning her mother's death. I wondered what the cause of her death was but, then I silently scolded myself for doing so. The girl was heartbroken, silently weeping over her mother's death. And I. I was thinking of the cause of her mother's death. Wow. How nice of me. I looked over at Oscar, taking in his god-like perfection. He stood there mystified, confusion spreading across his face like a highly contagious pandemic spreading across a country.

"Oscar, wha--"

"I. . . I can't believe it." he said, shaking his head. His eyes were starting to get red and tears were forming. I never imagined Oscar could cry. I mean, of course I knew that all humans could cry but he seemed tougher. Oscar took in a deep breath, wiping the tears before they could fall on his cheeks. "I need to be tough."
Oscar forced a smile.

"You can cry. I don't mind." I whispered. "Crying is a way to express yourself. There's no need to be ashamed of it."

"I. . ." Oscar started crying for real now. The big tears splotching down his face. It reminded me of rain. "Aunt Leila was so close to me. Every time I went over, she would greet me with a smile and fresh-baked cookies. She was like a second- mother to me. And I was like a son to her."

"Oh Oscar, it's. . . I'm so sorry." I said. I mean, what could I possibly say? "I know how it feels like. Honestly, I didn't have much time to cry or whatever. I need to tell my siblings that we were leaving. I really miss them. Both of them. My mom and my dad, but it's not like I can do anything about it now. We're somewhere in the cosmos now."

Oscar didn't answer. I couldn't blame him. In times like this, how were you possibly supposed to comfort a person when the news of a loved one's death was hitting them hard? Oscar left the tears silently fall down his face as he sat down on the nearby couch.

"Is Oscar crying?" screamed Gabrielle, now coming into view. Her butterscotch blonde hair was like a big yellow sun. A sun we no longer had. At least she doesn't have to worry about her hair becoming a black hole. "OMG! This is amazing!"

"Aunt Leila died," muttered Oscar his face like a blank board.

"Oh, really?" beamed Gabrielle, as she skipped toward us, a huge smile warming her face up. How could she be happy in such a time? "I never really liked Aunt Leila and the other Athertons. Only Cara. Cara was the best."

"She's six years older than you." mumbled Oscar, taking his head in his hands.

"Doesn't matter. She's the best." said Gabrielle, as she came closer to me. "As for you, I don't think you're making my brother feel any better, so please, out of our property."

"I don't think you're making him feel better, either," I said.

"Out of our property." snarled Gabrielle. How could she change herself from the sunny, happy, dancing girl to the outrageously rude tween? "I don't think you'll like being locked up by the Magistratus locking up in. A. Lonely. Cell."

Right. Imperium's excuse for police.

I rolled my eyes at Gabrielle, but she pretended not to notice anything. I edged toward the door, and saw Oscar's eyes follow my movement. I opened the door and stepped outside. The door slammed behind me. What was I to do now? I had no one to communicate with, no one to be with. I turned to my left walking down yet another endless hallway. The white walls with the blue stripes swished past me, the carpeted floor muffled my footsteps. I decided to get back to my chambers. It shouldn't have been far. I walked down another, and another, and another hallway and soon found myself in the hallway that contained all the other Star family chambers. I walked down the hallway and soon found the familiar door with our names on it. I opened it and walked inside. Our apartment looked exactly like the Smith's apartment. Copy-paste.

"Courtney? Dominik?" I yelled, wondering if my siblings had gone out as well.

Confused, I retreated to my room. Just as I was closing the door behind me, I heard a knock. I walked over to the front door and opened it, slightly annoyed at the person for I was just about to study a map of the Andromeda galaxy. I opened the door, surprised to find a stranger. He was Dominik's age, maybe a bit older, with brown hair, tanned skin, and hazel eyes. Nothing special. The boy smirked down at me.

"Is Courtney home?" he asked.

"No," I answered. "Why?"

"We were supposed to meet her but I see she had other plans."

"Who are you to her?" I asked.

"Kian Sparks." answered the boy. "Her boyfriend."

"Oh nice," I mused. "She did mention you a couple times."

"Funny, she never told me about you." said Kian. "She only told me about her 'annoying' twin brother Dominik."

"Oh well that's interesting. I'm her younger sister Luna."

"You look bored."

"I'm not though." I retorted.

Kian raised an eyebrow.

"You could probably hang out with my younger brother Jo and his girlfriend Liza." offered Kian. "They're a year younger than me."

"No thanks," I said. "I don't even know you. Or them for that matter."

Kian smirked at me but said nothing. I considered the idea. I *was* bored but, I didn't know Kian or his supposed brother and his supposed girlfriend. I wasn't sure I could trust him. But I had nothing to do. Life was all about taking measured risks.

"Sure," I told him. "I'll go."

Jo Sparks

"Hey Jo!" yelled a familiar voice. Kian.

"Let go of me!" yelled a female voice.

My brother's figure emerged, rom the doorway and I now clearly saw the girl. She was my age, had not brown but not blonde hair, she had ice blue eyes, and an intimidating snarl on her face. Kian was holding her by the elbow. What had he done?

"Kian, release the girl," ordered Liza, as she stood. "She's not your property."

"Of course, princess, I'll do whatever you say," mocked Kian as he bowed, letting go of the girl and pushing her into the wall in the process.

The girl hit the wall with a loud *THUD*! Liza rushed toward her, ignoring her half-finished Nutri.

"Kian, you better use manners! You know mom wouldn't like this!" I yelled.

"Keep your advice to yourself, Pipsqueak!" yelled Kian, as he strode off.

I ran over to where Liza was. The girl hissed in pain, and held her arm up to her chest. I saw a brace, and although it was supposed to protect her, she had apparently hit it.

"Oh how are you?" asked Liza, frantic. "Are you okay?"

"What's your name?" I asked. Liza shot me a hundred-dollar glare. Her amber eyes like gold. Her red hair like a flaming fireball around her.

"What's your name?" I asked again, keeping my distance from the girl.

"Luna Russell." she said, a big smile on her face. She had no pattern to her emotions, whatsoever. She was on an emotional rollercoaster. One second she was hissing in pain, the next second she dies, the next second she resurrects, and the next she's happy. "You must be Jo Sparks!"

"Indeed I am," I stammered, too surprised by her emotional change.

"And you are?"

"Liza King," said Liza, flashing a grin. "I've heard tons about you, Luna."

"Both your hair and eyes are incredibly pretty," said Luna. "Is that hair natural or dyed?"

"Um, natural," said Liza. Ugh, girl talk. I couldn't understand a thing. "And your hair is?"

"Natural."

The girls started talking, Luna obsessing over Astronomy, Astrology, and Cosmology and Liza obsessing over cliff diving, climbing, and the Hunger Games. I just stood there.

"Jo, why don't you join our conversation?" asked Liza, as she pulled me closer.

"You're talking about girl-things."

"We are not!" objected Liza.

"Astronomy and the Hunger Games are not girl talk! They're everyone talk!" said Luna.

"Fine," I said. I wasn't too psyched about this.

"What are your interests?" asked Liza. She already knew.

"I like wrestling." I automatically answered.

"Your favorite color?" asked Luna.

"Orange."

"Your favorite animal?" asked Luna, again. Her arm seemed to be doing better.

"A Bengal Tiger."

"They're extinct!" objected Liza.

"It doesn't matter. Luna, what's your favorite animal?"

"A Dodo bird,"

"It's extinct," I pointed out.

"No matter,"

We talked like this for a while, and I soon found that Luna's quirky and eccentric personality was fun to be around. She knew many things and was amazed when I shared my knowledge. Liza seemed to have made a new friend. We were all enjoying Luna's company and weren't surprised when she was part of a Star family. Although she acted very normal, Not like some of the other kids from prestige families. It startled me when my mom came through the door, a huge smile on her face.

"Hi Jo! Hi Liza!" she said, as she walked past us and settled herself onto the couch. "Who is your friend there?"

"Oh hello!" said Luna, as she rose from the floor where we were playing Monopoly. "I'm Luna Russell. You must be Mrs. Sparks!"

"Oh please! A Russell?" asked my mom, as she took off her high heels. "Russells are too prestige to ever visit us!"

"Mrs. Sparks, you must be thinking about my siblings." said Luna, as she sat back down now that it was her turn. "I don't think anyone is too prestige for me. Everyone is my equal."

"Huh. You are one weird Russell. Not like your selfish parents."

"What about my parents?"

"Your mom would never talk to anyone. She thought she was too important to talk to the lowly class. She was too full of herself when she became Dr. Marcy Brown's personal assistant." said my mom, as she focused her eyes on the Rbot 87 Max Glide. "Your dad thought he was so important being the head manager of the meteorology sector."

"Mom, stop this!" I said, as I saw Luna getting uncomfortable. No doubt she wouldn't want to spend time with us if my mom despised her. Gritting my teeth and taking in a deep breath, I tried to refrain myself from being mad at my mom for this. "Don't you see? She's not like them!"

"Oh well, that's too good," said my mom as she scrolled down something that would probably be Facebook. "Those stupid, irresponsible,--"

Luna stood up and headed to the door. Before she left, she turned to us and said, "Thank you for your company, friends. I had a splendid time. I will now go, as I can see I'm not entirely welcomed."

Luna turned and walked out of the room.

Liza King

I stood there, stunned, unable to move for a few moments. Wow, Jo's mom was rude. Wasn't she aware that other people in the world had emotions as well? Obviously not. I looked at Jo once again mesmerized by his greenish-yellowish eyes and unruly black hair. He was so full of imperfections yet everything seemed perfect about him, if that makes any sense. He met my gaze and we shared a moment of sadness. Luna had such an eccentric personality, it was sad to see her go. I stood up and ran out of the apartment in hopes of catching up to Luna. Jo bounded after me.

"Be back by morning!" yelled Jo's mom after us. Yeah, right. I wanted to see the control room, to climb the pipes and lose myself.

"Where're we going?" asked Jo, as he caught up with me. "Where do you think she went?"

"Well, considering that both our families are only bronze tier, she might've gone to the gold tier section." I explained. In Imperium, everyone was in a class. Star families were the most honored families. Bronze tier were the least honored and gold tier were the most honored. Silver was obviously in between. Not many people were silver tier. The only silver tiered people I knew about were the Zimmermans.

We turned a corner and were soon on the elevators, leading up to the gold tier section. The doors opened and before us spread a larger hallway, more lavish and elaborate. It still had a patterned carpet, put fancy chandeliers hung from the ceiling. As we walked out, we slowed our pace to keep away from any rising suspicion.

Soon, we came to the door marked *Russell Family*. Jo knocked on the door, and our gazes met. Luna might be mad at us. But, why would she? I didn't have time to consider before someone opened the door.

In front of me was a girl older than Luna. She was so unlike Luna. She had golden blonde hair and deep blue eyes. They reminded me of the ocean on a good day. Some of her mascara was smeared but in ways, she still looked good. She was wearing a crop top and the shortest jean shorts I had ever seen. She looked sixteen maybe older but otherwise, my age.

"Who are you?" she asked us, a smirk distorting her otherwise beautiful face.

"I'm Liza King and this is Jo Sparks." I said, with a smile. "We're friends of Luna's and we were wondering if she stopped by this. . . um apartment."

"That's interesting. Luna doesn't have friends," said the girl as she slammed the door on our faces. Well, that was hospitable. I turned to Jo. He was leaning against the wall, obviously concentrating.

"Where would she go?" I asked Jo as I walked over beside him.

"I don't know." said Jo, as he checked his wrist. "But it's three in the morning and the Magistratus will be patrolling." Jo shuddered. "We don't want to get locked up in a cell for wandering during night hours."

I frowned.

I didn't mind wandering. Honestly, I loved wandering. It was a way in which I could explore the possibilities of new places. But Jo was right to some extent. I could climb the pipes later. I could visit the archery pitch later. I wouldn't be able to do those things if I got locked up, now would I? I nodded and stood up. Together we walked to our bedrooms, avoiding all main corridors in which the Magistratus might find us.

Two weeks later. . .
Nova Osborne

I walked down the white hallways, dragging my suitcase behind me. It was going to be a long day. Ever since I boarded the Urania 2.7 I had been dreading the day I would have to board the Super Astra. The day the rest of the world would see my face. I was a new individual starting all over. I was Nova Estelle Osborne. Daughter of Arabelle and Sebastian

Osborne. My supposed parents were the founders of Osborne and Co.- a publishing company that the real Arabelle and Sebastian actually founded.

I took a deep breath and continued moving through the ship. I hoped I wouldn't meet anyone who knew me as Whitney Stone. Then things would be tragic.

"All passengers must board the Super Astra immediately." warned the artificial female voice through invisible speakers. This voice had been blaring through the ship for the past two days, ever since those girls Venus, Oceane, and Noelle bored us to death with a lecture about all the things on the Uranium. They had failed pretty badly since the silences between them handing the microphone over were long. They would mess up often, and had to be re-directed by their manager. "This ship be will self-destruct in forty- three minutes and 18 seconds. . . 17 seconds. . . 16 seconds. . . 15 seconds. All passengers please follow exit signs for your section. I repeat. All passengers please follow exit signs for your section."

How pleasant. The ship would self-destruct. For a moment, I considered staying on the ship. Then, I wouldn't have to see all the people that knew me as Whitney Stone.

I walked through yet another white, sterile, chemical-smelling hallway. Ugh. They could've used something more pleasant for the human nose. I felt like I was in a hospital.

A couple passed me, their hands tangled up in one another, making goo-goo eyes at each other. Well, one of them, or maybe both, were going to be heartbroken pretty soon. Love was nonsense. It was like a dictator. Once you fall under its control it dictates everything you do. If and when you break out, you suffer the consequences of your foolishness. Love at first sight was a bunch of nonsense that made Hollywood billions of dollars. Love was like a devil, sweet when it wanted to be and cruel and heart-rending when it felt like toying with you like a cat with its prey.

I rounded a corner and sure enough, a large sign with animated letters said *Dock 91*. Perfect. Now when we reached the Super Astra, I would be one of the first people to board it. I would then hide in my room and no one would ever know that I existed.

The dream caught me off guard and I soon crashed into someone. I heard a slight yelp, and scolded myself for being caught off guard. Surely, the person would've saw me. And recognized me.

I opened my eyes to see a younger girl steadying her duffle bag. Great, I would escape, once and for all. I took a step to the left, but my conscience kicked in. *How dare you, Whitney? No, not Whitney. How dare you, Nova? You crashed into someone. It's only nice to say sorry. It's only right.* Stupid conscience. I turned around and said, "I'm so sorry. I wasn't watching where I was going. Are you alright?"

The girl looked at me and I was astonished by her beauty. She had hair that was impossible to distinguish. It wasn't brown, but it wasn't dirty blonde either. The sharpness of her ice-blue eyes pierced me through like a knife through hot butter but, the glare I expected, was smothered by her kind expression. She gave me a smile, then said, "I'm just as good as you are." What was that supposed to mean? Whatever it meant, it gave no comfort to me at all. "What's your name? You don't look much older than me."

She was right. The girl looked like she was fourteen. I was fifteen.

"Whi-Nova." I said. Whew, that was close. "I'm fifteen. And you?"

"Oh, my name is Luna Russell and I'm fourteen. Did you know that you look a lot like my brother Dominik's girlfriend, Whinova?"

A Russell.

Out of all the people in the world, I crashed into a Russell that found out who I was.

Really?

My luck could not have been any worse.

"Oh, um, my name's not Whinova. It's just Nova" I said, schooling my expression. "And no, I didn't know that I looked like your brother's girlfriend."

"Interesting." said Luna, her mind in a far-away world.

"Luna stop wasting time, or we'll leave you here!" yelled a voice that made me uncomfortable. A very familiar voice. Too familiar. I turned toward the sound and saw. . . him. Dominik was marching toward Luna, his sister Courtney right behind him. I turned away, looking for a chance to flee. I started walking away but stopped in mid step.

"Whitney?" asked Dominik, his voice full of wonder and disgust. "Is that really you?"

I had been uncovered.

Luna Russell

"Oh that's where I recognized her from!" I exclaimed, comparing a mental image of Whitney Stone and this girl Nova. They were identical. The same curly black hair, the same pitch-black eyes. She had the same big eyelashes, outlined with mascara. She was the same person, or so I thought. The Nova-girl turned to stare at my brother, and he stared back, his eyes full of shock. The Nova-girl shook her head in disgust and speed-walked on, the suitcase behind her bouncing up and down at her speed.

"Whitney, wait!" yelled my brother as he sped after her. "I know it was wrong, but wait!"

"So much for being early," muttered Courtney, as she fixed the zippers on her suitcase. I shot her a glare. We could still go in the Super Astra. We didn't have to wait for Dominik to get back from his love-chase. "I'm not waiting for him."

"But Courtney, he'll get lost." I said. "He's not good in the head."

"You aren't good in the head, either," said Courtney, as she stood up. "I'm going inside. Come if you want."

"But Dominik--"

"Dominik can take care of himself, Luna." said Courtney, as she took a step forward. "You know mom and dad wouldn't be proud of you."

"You can't say that." I growled, now mad at Courtney for being so negative. Mom was always proud of me. As for Dad. . . I couldn't say. "How do you know?"

"I just do, Luna." said Courtney, as she walked away from me, heading toward the tunnel leading to the Super Astra. A large smile was on her face, as she chuckled to herself. I was furious. So I set off to find Dominik.

I set off in the direction I had last seen Dominik going. I walked on and on, tugging my suitcase and duffle bag behind me. After all, Courtney always acted like a jerk. I shouldn't be mad about it now. I made my way through the dense batch of people before me, and I saw them. I had no idea how far away we were from the ship. Whitney/Nova and Dominik were by the escort-robot charging stations. Whitney/Nova looked like she was crying. Dominik's expression changed much too quickly for me to see if he was apologizing or mad. I edged closer trying decipher what was happening. I edged closer and closer to them, close enough to overhear their conversation. For a moment, I felt bad about eavesdropping on them but the feeling vanished when I heard their conversation.

"I don't know who you are." said Whitney/Nova. She was obviously stressed about something but I couldn't figure out what that something was. "My name is Nova Osborne, and I don't appreciate you following me around saying that I'm this Whitney. I have no idea what you're talking about."

"But of course you do! It's you, and I know it!" said Dominik as he edged closer to Whitney/Nova. "You can't possibly have a clone!"

"Don't touch me!" hissed Whitney/Nova as she shoved my brother away from her. "I will call the Magistratus on you if I must. Stop bothering me with your nonsense."

"But it's you!"

"What would you do if I'm this Whitney?"

"I would tell her I love her and that I'm sorry."

Whitney Nova snorted but turned away from Dominik.

"I have no idea what happened between you and this Whitney but let me tell you something. I don't think she wants your supposed love."

"But I--"

"You have feelings for another girl, let me guess."

My brother considered this for a moment, and then slowly said, "It's none of your business if you aren't Whitney. But I know you're Whitney. You may change your name to Nova Osborne. You may feed me false stories about you being the daughter of Arabelle and Sebastian Osborne but I know the truth. You are Whitney. My Whitney. And I'm about to call the Magistratus on you."

Dominik raised his wrist to his mouth, and started speaking. Crap, he was actually calling the Magistratus. If they didn't find any evidence, he would be locked up in a cell for suspicion of betrayal.

"Magistratus, what crime are you to report?" asked an unfamiliar male voice.

"I believe I have found---"

"No!" I yelled, as I raced toward them. Cassie jumped off my shoulder, her claws tearing into my shoulder blade. Whitney/Nova looked at me with surprise. Dominik glared at me with murderous eyes.

"Ah baby sister!" mused Dominik, as he tapped his wrist. Turning the sound off, I guessed. "What are you doing here?"

"Dominik, if she says she's not Whitney, then she's not Whitney. Her name is Nova," I said, as I speed-walked toward them. Getting closer and closer with every step. "There's no need to call the Magistratus over her not being Whitney."

"In fact there is. I believe I have found Tiffany Ciapponi."

The name stopped me in my tracks.

Tiffany Ciapponi.

The famed child criminal.

Just because her parents were Ruby Cox and Ethan Ciapponi- the world famous murderers, she was registered as a potentially dangerous criminal. Even though, she had done nothing. I always thought that this decision was very rash of Imperium to do so. The girl didn't pick who she was born to. The girl was innocent. Innocent.

I looked at Whitney/Nova. Her face was pale as snow.

"So you believe you have found Tiffany Ciapponi?" I asked, now resuming my speed-walk.

"Yes." said Dominik as he smiled smugly. Whitney/Nova tried to run but Dominik held her firmly by the arm.

"And what evidence points you to that conclusion?" I asked. I now felt like one of the Magistratus. Too bossy.

"She is Whitney Stone. Tiffany Ciapponi changed her name to Whitney Stone once the world knew who she was." Dominik explained, now holding the struggling Whitney/Nova with both hands. "Whitney Stone, apparently changed her name to Nova Osborne, after I broke up with her. All evidence points her to be guilty."

"Guilty of what?"

"Her parents are criminals, Luna!"

"So what? Just because her parents are criminals, that makes her a criminal, too? That's pretty stupid, Dominik. We don't choose who our parents are. And it's not her fault that they're criminals. She didn't do anything wrong." I retorted. "If you think she's Whitney, I need to ask you a question. Do you love Whitney?"

"Love? No!" snorted Dominik.

"But you just said--"

"Sush, Whitney."

"Then does it make a difference if she changes her name to avoid you or if she gets into prison for something she didn't do?"

"Yes, I rather not see her at all."

"So it doesn't make a difference?"

Dominik considered this for a moment.

"No, it doesn't."

"Great! Hand her over to me, and I'll make sure you never cross paths again." I explained as Dominik pushed Whitney/ Nova toward me. I barely caught her. "Don't you dare call the Magistratus, Dominik. Let's make a deal. If I make sure you don't cross paths again, will you promise not to call the Magistratus on her?"

"No, I could get tons of money!"

I glared at Dominik.

"Dominik, you know very well that she did nothing wrong. And its unfair to be held responsible for what her parents did. She just wants to live a normal life and not to be haunted because of her parent's bad reputation."

"Alright, alright. If she never crosses paths with me again, I will not call the Magistratus on her."

"Great." I said, as I turned around heading toward my abandoned suitcase. "Let's go, Nova."

Oscar Smith

"The Smith Star family chambers," said Percy, the guy from room service as he presented a door with *Smith Star Family* inscripted into the cypress wood. Alexander snorted in disgust behind me, and Gabrielle squealed. She's babbled all about the premium features of the Super Astra, bouncing from one side of the hallway to the other the whole time. My mind wandered, and I thought about Luna, how kind she had been, and how Gabrielle threatened to call the Magistratus if she didn't get out of our apartment. I was too weak by the smell of blood. It smelled so much like iron, it made me sick. I was light headed and couldn't think properly. Once I got better I realized what I had let Gabrielle do. I felt horrible. Luna was just trying to comfort me. A growl built up in my chest, and I couldn't hold it in. My growl startled Percy. He took a step back and covered his face to hide his horrified expression.

"Mr-Mr. Smith, a- are you okay?" stammered Percy, as he took his face out of his hands, his face pale and scared. "Is there anything I could do to help you? Perhaps take you to the psychiatrist?"

"No, Percy, that will not be necessary. I will go explore the ship." I announced.

"Leaving without seeing your room?" asked Percy, his face still etched with worry lines. "Are you going to see all the Urania spaceships self-destruct?"

"No." I answered. I didn't understand why Percy was still horrified by me. I was perfectly normal. Well, sort of normal. "I will go explore the ship."

I turned around and walked down a hallway. These hallways were much more hospitable than the one's on the Urania. These hallways were painted light orange so the lights created a cozy glow when turned on. The carpet was cream colored. Everything was so nice in the gold tier Star family section but, who knows what the conditions were in the Normalem sections. The normal sections. Where normal people stayed. Everything that I had seen in the Super Astra was made so that it projected hospitality, warmth, and comfort. Everything was made for a long-term journey, and the thought made me uncomfortable. Although the travel time was to be reduced 99.99% (since we were traveling faster than light) it would still be a good two to three years until we even got to another galaxy. A galaxy with a Sun. A galaxy with a planet able to sustain human life.

As I walked farther and farther from my apartment, I tried to picture the fact that two billion people were aboard this spaceship. It was hard to picture. My thought swam back to Luna, her piercingly beautiful ice blue eyes, her warm smile, and the kindness she always projected. I pictured how I'd last seen her. She'd been wearing a flannel shirt, black fuzzy leggings and teal sneakers. She'd been dressed so casual, yet she looked like a princess.

I walked down the hallway making up my mind. I would find Luna and apologize for what I let Gabrielle do. I ventured down the hallway. Percy had mentioned that there were two gold tier Star family sections since the highest ranked people in the country deserved to have space. If the Russell family was in my section, I would know. The Russell family must be in the other section. I sped toward the next connecting hallway, speeding past crew members giving Star families tours of the ship. They all gave me disapproving looks but that didn't stop me. I needed to see Luna. I wanted to see Luna. It was top priority.

I kept on speed-walking and soon found myself sprinting. I relieved when I finally came to the other gold tier Star family section. I slowed down, catching my breath, and fixing my hair. I needed to look presentable for Luna. I walked down the hallway, and soon found a door similar to mine, labeled *Russell Star Family*. I let out a shaky breath in relief. Wait, what if Luna was mad at me? She didn't seem like the type but, still, I worried. I inhaled another shaky breath and rung the doorbell. I waited a couple moments, my nerves frazzling like electric wires. I heard footsteps and let out a surge of carbon dioxide. The door opened.

"Luna?" I asked in disbelief. Her face was painted with a large smile that warmed me up from head to toe.

"Oh Oscar!" she exclaimed, as she ushered me inside.

Luna Russell

Oscar stepped inside the apartment, too stunned to say anything. I settled him on the couch near the holographic fireplace. The apartment was like the one we had on the Urania, just with more features. We had a premium holographic fireplace, two bathrooms, a storage tank, and an exercise center with the holograph of this woman doing random exercises. Perfect for Courtney.

"Oh Oscar, I haven't seen you in a long time," I said, amazed to see him here. I always thought he was mad at me. The thought hurt me to some extent.

"You're not mad at me?" asked Oscar. He still looked confused but he looked better than before.

"No! Why would I be?" I asked, confused at his question. There was no reason for me to still be mad at him.

"Well, Gabrielle kicked you out and I didn't do anything to stop her."

"You were weak, pale, and. . . did I say weak?" Honestly, ever since I was kicked out of the Smith's apartment, I'd been having trouble with my memory. Perhaps Science had turned against me. Oscar flinched violently.

"I wanted to stop Gabrielle, honestly, but-"

"You were weak, that's all. I'm not mad at you. I have no reason to be mad at you." I reasoned. "You were hurt."

We sat in silence for a while, eyeing the little details of the living room. My mind wandered to how the girl Evelyn Atherton had told Oscar that her mother was dead. It had torn him apart. He seemed fine now, but I could see right through him. He was a bad liar. The fact that this Leila Atherton had died, still bothered him like a wound that had just gotten a scab. Picking at it would make it open up and ooze again.

Courtney was in the exercise room and Dominik was out meeting friends. Nova was sleeping in one of the extra bedrooms. We were alone. All alone. So. . . nah, I wouldn't say it was romantic. Okay, maybe a little.

"The Athertons." said Oscar, as he suddenly jumped up. "I forgot we're all on the same ship, now. We should go see Bella, and Lauren, and. . . Evelyn. . . and Cara."

I suspected that this Bella girl was more than a friend but I kept my mouth shut. I wrote a note to Nova on my WrisPlay.

I'm out with a friend. Don't worry, I'll be back by ten. There's some pasta in the fridge. Stay out of Dominik's way and only go out of the room when he's not around. Be safe.

I then followed Oscar out of the room.

Oscar held the door open for me and it made butterflies flutter in my stomach. How kind and sweet the gesture was. Oscar lead me through a series of never-ending hallways until we found a holographic map with all the family names in the place their apartment was. We searched for a long time, trying to find the Athertons with no luck. Finally, the name showed itself. It was located on the western side of floor eighteen. It wasn't far from here. We ventured down yet another hallway, in unbearable silence. How charming he was when he talked. We climbed down a maze of stairs and soon found ourselves on floor eighteen. This was the Normalem section- where the normal people lived. I always wanted to live here, because here people were normal, and when other people passed them, they didn't give them a second thought. Being part of one of the most honored families in Imperium was too much for my liking. Here the walls were painted a dull grey and the carpet was black. Lights flickered on and off above my head sending a hostile and unwelcome feeling throughout the hallway.

We wandered the hallway and soon found a door labeled *Atherton Family*. Oscar knocked on the door with a muscular hand. I found my thoughts dawdling and scolded myself. *Luna, what are you doing? Stop this instant! You'll get into trouble!* I silently told my conscience to shut up.

Just then, the door opened and a girl older than me appeared. She was eighteen, nineteen, maybe twenty. She had flowing honey blonde hair, dark grey eyes, and was tall. Very tall. She wore grey sweatpants, a grey sweater, and grey socks. She had mascara, although it was smeared as if she'd been crying. No doubt, crying over her dead mother. The thought made me feel ill. My own mother was dying or dead back on Earth. I was an orphan. I looked back at the girl. Everything about her was grey, except her hair. She was beautiful, in her own way.

"Hello Lauren." said Oscar, in a dark and depressing voice. "I heard about Aunt Leila. I'm so sorry." The Lauren girl remained silent. "We though we might visit you."

"C'mon in," she whispered. I followed Oscar into the apartment. Unlike, my apartment, this one was normal. It had electric heaters instead of holographic fireplaces, it had a tiled floor that made the room feel hostile, and cream colored walls. It was shaped similarly to the apartment the Star families had aboard the Urania. Just not as much detail and comfort.

On the couch, a girl sat with a nearly empty box of tissues next to her. She was wiping tears away from her face. She had shoulder length golden hair and stunning green eyes. She was skinny but still slightly muscular and like Evelyn, was short. On the floor sat another girl. I recognized her. This was Evelyn. She wore the same dark and depressed expression as before, but now she was sobbing. Leaning against the wall with an annoyed expression was a girl that looked like Evelyn's clone. She even had Evelyn's soft blue eyes.

"This is Evelyn." said Lauren as she pointed to Evelyn. "And Bella." she said as she pointed to the couch girl. "And Cara."

Cara turned out to be Evelyn's clone. Twins, I supposed. I looked over at Oscar. He seemed distraught at this scene. I felt like I was at a funeral. I realized Lauren was introducing the sisters to me and I scolded myself for being so slow. Oscar went and sat down with Bella, comforting her. She looked at him, her eyes full of tears. He said something to comfort her again, and she resumed her sobbing. They were crying over their mom. I on the other hand, was upset, but I never cried over losing my mom. Okay, I cried once. Maybe we weren't that close. Actually, we weren't that close but still, I should've been mourning her. I decided I should try to comfort them. I scooted closer to Evelyn, but she snarled at me, creating an evident message that I wasn't welcomed. I tried comforting Bella but, Oscar was already doing that and I couldn't interfere. Cara needed no comforting and Lauren just sat there faceless, motionless, emotionless.

The atmosphere around me became heavy and depressing. Just as I was about to leave to get some fresh air, Oscar announced that we should get going. I jumped up and nearly ran to the door with relief. Evelyn glared daggers at me, and Lauren stared at me with disgust. Cara was painting her nails. Only Bella seemed too busy sobbing to notice me. I opened the door and to my surprise, found the unfriendly hallway comforting. At least it didn't contain three girls mourning their mother's death.

We walked down the hallway in silence. I noticed that Oscar was quietly crying as well. I wondered if people were just very sensitive or if I didn't feel emotion like normal people.

Bella Atherton

Aunt Malena had always told me that crying was a way to express your feelings. I had never cried so much in my life. I don't think I cried so much when I was an infant. The feelings that were surging out of my body now were indescribable. Depression, sadness, anger, and more just flooded out of me. As if I was an overfilled tank that wouldn't stop getting filled. I would overflow again and again and again. Oscar had comforted me a little, but he had left with the girl he brought. I was happy for him. He brought a girl, meaning he had a girlfriend. I sighed. I had never thought of Oscar as more than a childhood friend but, maybe just maybe I was starting to develop feelings for him. Though they were slight, I still want us to stay friends. Nothing more, nothing less. That girl sure was lucky. Oscar was a nice guy.

I looked around the room. Evelyn lay sprawled spread eagle on the cold tile floor. She shuddered every time she breathed no doubt, remembering our mother's lifeless body. She was the one who got the news. She was the one to see my mother's lifeless body getting moved to the morgue. I felt bad for her. It must've been horrible. I didn't get the news until I boarded the Super Astra.

I looked around to see Lauren, silently weeping in a corner. She was huddled into a ball, her shoulders shaking from her tears. Lauren had been attending college in California. She would soon resume her education aboard the Super Astra, just like the rest of us would. Lauren wanted to be a forensic scientist. The demand for that job was high and if she achieved it, she'd be really rich. I, on the other hand, wanted to be a medical scientist. I wanted to learn where all the viruses and infections came from.

I looked around one more time to see Cara fixing her manicure. She wore wireless headphones and was probably listening to music. The thought that my older sister didn't care if our mother was dead or alive sickened me. Cara lived with her friend Darla Frost. She seemed happier.

She was just visiting now. She never came to Iceland to visit. Even when Aunt Malena said she would pay her airplane ticket, Cara didn't come.

I looked down to the pile of dirty tissues at my feet. I was no doubt, a mess. I stood up, and headed toward the doorway. No one looked at me. No one noticed me. They were all in their mourning world. I made up my mind. I would go see Liza King. She was better friends with Evelyn, but I ignored that fact. Liza had lost her best friend, Angelica Howell, to murder. She would know how to fix me. How to repair the broken pieces of my soul, if they could be repaired at all.

All I knew was that after Angelica's unexpected murder, Liza had fallen into deep depression. She'd fixed it by rock climbing. She let her emotions out through her climbing. She'd overcome her depression and now had a free adventurous spirit, and a boyfriend- Jo Sparks. Liza was two years older than me, sixteen. She'd lost her friend when she was nine. She should know how to fix me to some extent.

I opened the door and walked out into the hostile hallway with hope, a tiny thing fluttering in my chest. Maybe, just maybe I could get out of this fire unscathed.

Liza King

I heard a knock. A half-hearted, barely heard, but still desperate knock. Desperate for help. Or something else.

"Go get it, Liza!" called my father as he lay on the couch. He'd been very exhausted during the past few days, mainly because he was the captain of the Urania 2.7. He had to pilot day and night, not that you could tell day and night apart. Outer space was always dark. I rushed to the door. I didn't want to busy my mother, either. She'd been at all the advertisement meetings with Jo's mom. I opened the door and saw a strangely familiar girl standing in the doorway. I couldn't figure out where I knew her from.

The girl had shoulder length golden hair with stunning emerald green eyes. She was so unlike me. I had red hair down to my waist and amber eyes. So unlike this fragile girl standing in the doorway. In a way, she reminded me of Angelica. Angelica had had pitch black hair but the same stunning green eyes. The girl wore a pair of skinny jeans and a purple sweatshirt. Her hair was a mess.

"Hello, you're Liza King, right?" whispered the girl. She looked even more fragile when she talked.

"Yes, and you are?"

"Bella Atherton,"

The name turned on an alarm in my head. The Athertons. I should've known. I used to be friends with Evelyn. They were nice to us, and we were nice to them. Everything had been fine, before Angelica had been murdered. After she died, I fell into deep depression and distanced myself from the other friends I had. I hadn't been to the Atherton's house since I was nine. They knew I had lost someone, they knew I was in deep depression, but did they do something to help me? No. They just distanced themselves away from me, pretended they never knew me.

I suspected the mother- Leila, being behind this because her children, were children. Lauren was fourteen. She had other friends and never really played with me or whatever, so she couldn't have been behind it. But Leila had always been so sweet, always making us cookies and whatnot. And now, Bella Atherton was standing in my doorway. What was I to do? Slam the door in her face? That would be rude.

"C'mon in, Bella."

Bella nodded and came in. She looked like the living dead. Something really must be bothering her. I lead her to my room that way we wouldn't disrupt my parents.

"Why are you here, Bella?" I asked.

Bella stayed silent for a long time.

"My mom died." she whispered, her voice quavering the whole time.

I didn't know what to say. It was hard to imagine that sweet, kind, caring Leila would have died. When did this happen? What caused her death? Questions were flooding my brain. I looked over at Bella, and realized that she was silently weeping. Her shoulders were shaking and her hands were trembling. I scooted closer to Bella, and ignored the foreign feeling rising in my throat as I wrapped an arm around her to comfort her. Really, I didn't know what to say. Everyone takes death differently. Some fall into depression, others get suicidal, other people are sad but don't get depressed or suicidal, and there are exceptions when people celebrate or don't care about a person's death.

With a jolt, I realized that Cara must be an exception. I had never been fond of her, because of her bratty demeanor.

I pushed that thought away, and started comforting Bella in every way I could. If I knew something about death, it would be that death could break you to pieces. I would hold Bella together for as long as I could. She could get out of hell unharmed, if I walked next to her. If I was her support.

And together, we walked through hell.

I looked at the inside of my wrist, scrolling through the news articles, but unaware of their contents or topics. Nothing mattered right now. I was numb. Too numb to care for anything. As I scrolled down further I noticed a headline, outlined in bright yellow.

Mysterious Purple Ring Appears on Teen's Shoulder, Teen Dies 24 Hours Later-Article #5

I held my breath as I tapped on the article, bracing myself for the worst.

Fifteen year old, Jason Harpwood, son of Serenity and Maverick Harpwood dies from unknown disease. The teen noticed a small, purple ring on his shoulder. This was unusual and unnerving therefore, Jason Harpwood was admitted to the hospital where he was treated with antibiotics. The next morning, Jason Harpwood was found dead. He had similar purple rings all over his body.
"It was quite unnerving. This is something you don't see everyday." commented Dr. Florence Coleman, Head of the Department of Health. "It was horrible. I will personally lead an investigation to find out more about this deadly disease. For now we know nothing about this disease. We can only hope that we will find a cure to the 'Death Fever'."

Dr. Florence Coleman's full interview can be found on Article #6
Serenity and Maverick Harpwood's full interview can be found on Article #7
Symptoms of the 'Death Fever' can be found on Article #8

I tapped out of the article horrified.

Christabelle Carey- President of Imperium

"Gullery, how did this happen?" I asked, as I looked at the lifeless bodies, sprawled all over the cafeteria floor. Hundreds of thousands of people died. More were joining them. Some of the most important people in Imperium had died in the hands of Mortemisis. Mortemisis, the Death Fever, spread around the ship like wildfire. You'd die within days of contracting it, and the symptoms always showed up two days before you lost your life, so no one could know if they had contracted Mortemisis until that person's last days of life. Dr. Marcy Brown had died of Mortemisis a couple hours ago, leaving her son Jacob in the care of his absent father. Gabrielle Smith of the Smith Star family had died of Mortemisis two days ago. Courtney Russell of the Russell Star family had died yesterday. Kian Sparks of the Sparks Star family died three days ago.

Everyone was dying. My own daughter, Melanie, had contracted the disease from her father who died mere days before she was diagnosed with Mortemisis. People from the Normalem sectors were dying so frequently that no one bothered to have funerals anymore. There were just too many lifeless bodies that needed to be thrown into space. It wasn't even safe here, on the balcony overlooking the cafeteria. So high up, yet so close to death. Mortemisis was everywhere. A pandemic killing off the world I had worked so hard to create. We didn't know what caused it, just that it was spreading too fast for anyone to do something about it. I looked over at Gullery who had lost his sister *and* his girlfriend to the disease.

"Why is this happening?"

"I can't say, Mrs. Carey," said Gullery, as he bowed when he noticed I had looked at him. "Is there anything I could do to ensure your comfort, Mistress Carey? Tea, perhaps?"

"No Gullery, that will be all. Thank you," I whispered, my eyes locked on the hundreds of thousands of dead bodies sprawled on the floor. The med-droids came in with yet another body on the stretcher. Dayonara King, wife of Mark King and mother of Liza King. She was the head of the political board of directors. I knew her well. She was a childhood friend. And now, she was dead. My Dayonara was dead. I crumbled onto the floor, kaleidoscopes appearing in my eyes as I cried my heart out.

Luna Russell

I crouched near my bed, unaware of my surroundings. I was numb. Too numb to feel anything. Sure, Courtney had been a jerk to me my whole life, but I loved her dearly, and now I had lost her to Mortemisis. To Death himself. I recalled the memory of Courtney laying there, on the med-bed, all shriveled up and purple. In her last days of life, she asked me to tell Dominik that she loved him. Dominik, hadn't come during Courtney's last days, for he was weeping over the death of Evelyn Atherton. Evelyn had died a few days before Courtney.

I wasn't there when Evelyn had her last breath but I could tell that last breath was a painful one by the way Dominik weeped when he came home. I was afraid Dominik could do something stupid, but now it was my time to mourn. When we left our mom, I had been to busy with Courtney and Dominik's daily drama to mourn properly. Dominik was almost seventeen. Surely, he could do without my supervision. I needed time to mourn. Courtney had taken a part of me with her. I no longer had someone to be constantly annoyed with. Dominik was constantly weeping and out of the house. I was always lonely. I didn't go to see my friends. Liza had lost her mom. Oscar had lost Gabrielle. Bella had lost Evelyn. Jo had lost Kian. Everyone had lost someone. I didn't want to inflict my grief upon them. They all had enough grief to deal with.

Oscar Smith

I entered what was Gabrielle's room. It still contained pink posters of puppies on the wall and pink bedclothes. It still contained her strawberry scented perfume. The sight filled me with sadness but it was the only place I could still feel her presence. Her friends came by the day, begging to leave bouquets of flowers on her bed. Each day we would throw them out, to eliminate any chances of contracting Mortemisis ourselves. Alexander didn't seem to weep much. He just stood there with a blank, expressionless face. I knew Gabrielle's death had taken a toll on him as well. My mom had started drinking and was often at the pub. My dad had started working day and night. He basically lived at the NASA research center. I knew losing a child must be horrible. Losing Gabrielle had taken a toll on the whole family.

My mind was often wandering left and right. I thought about Jo, Bella, and Liza, how they were coping with their loses. But I mostly thought about Luna. It was hard to picture that a perfect girl could grieve and mourn. Every time I pictured Luna, crying by her bed, I pushed that thought away, before I would start weeping. I didn't want Luna to suffer. But there was nothing I could do to ease her grief when I was deep in the abyss myself.

Jo Sparks

My mom walked past me, but she was nothing more than a slowly moving outline of a person. The cold wall made my mind freeze. My eyesight fogged. I hadn't gone to Liza's house, she hadn't gone to my house. I thought everything was for the best. I missed Liza every second of every day, but for the moment, I missed Kian more. My bratty excuse for a brother had been nothing more than a nuisance but deep down, I loved him so much. Everyone seemed to be in a trance. My mom never spoke, my dad would cook which was not normal for him. And I, I got sucked into depression. Slowly. . . slowly. . . slowly.

Liza King

I walked aimlessly around the room not knowing what I was doing. Mom would cheer us up. But mom wasn't here. She was in a better place. Maybe that place had a Sun. Maybe her dead friends were there as well. Or maybe she was suffering for all the bio-engineering she had ever done. Although she worked as the head of the board of directors, my mom had been a research scientist.

She had bio-engineered many things, using the genes of an Iranian cucumber and the genes of a Fuji apple to create a softer apple. An apple that not even the elderly would have trouble eating. She'd crossed the genes of a rat and a crocodile to create a fearsome warrior for the Third World War. She'd done the same to people. She'd crossed human genes with the genes of a grizzly bear. The outcome-America's fierce warriors.

Everyone had been caused so much pain by her creations. Everyone.

I missed Jo, but I knew by going to his house, I would inflict my pain upon him. He would inflict his upon me. I could not, and would not stand it. I sat down on the cold floor and willed myself to sleep.

Bella Atherton

I sighed, and looked up at the picture of Evelyn hanging on the wall. I had never been close to my sister, especially since I had gone to live with Aunt Malena when I was four. Evelyn, like Cara, had never visited me. The only person who visited me was Lauren and she did that years ago.

Evelyn's death had been a shock, especially since it came right after the news of our mom's death. I remember Evelyn just going out, staying overnight somewhere. The Magistratus had found her in a hallway three floors above us. They had escorted her to the apartment and had made us pay an abnormally large sum of money. Two days later, we'd found her shriveled and purple in her bed. Dead.

Although Evelyn's death took me by surprise, I never really mourned her. Yes, I was sad, but I had no vivid memory of her. I didn't know what she looked like until now. We hadn't seen each other, Cara and Evelyn had been busy. They hadn't remembered they had a little sister living in Iceland. Though, Cara had been brutally rude, Evelyn wasn't the kindest person either.

I felt weird being around Lauren. She would weep for Evelyn *and* mom. Yes, I was still sad about losing mom, but like Cara and Evelyn, she never came to visit. I wasn't extremely close to her. Connections and relationships aren't the same when online.

I looked around the kitchen once again. I missed my friends. I missed Liza, Jo, Oscar, and Luna. I missed Luna the most. Her quirky personality could lighten anyone's mood. But I knew that Luna was mourning Courtney. She probably couldn't enlighted her own mood.

Everyone looked so gloomy. I would pass weeping people in the hallways, see people weeping in the control stations instead of doing their work. Christabelle Carey, President of Imperium had been weeping all day over losing her best friend- Dayonara King, her husband, and her three year-old daughter Melanie. I wanted to go see my friends, but I couldn't.

The sadness of my losses had already faded. There was a faint, hollow feeling over losing my mother, but like with Evelyn, my mother had rarely been there for me. I had nothing to grieve about. I could do nothing as my friends were drowning in sorrow's waters. My help wasn't welcomed. They would see that I wasn't mourning anyone. They would plunge deeper as they saw that they were in such a bad situation. I had nothing. No one. I was by myself. It was me against the grieving world.

Nova Osborne

I lay in Luna's room, watching all the mini models of planets spin as the air conditioner threw up gust of cold air. Cassie was purring in the corner on the bed next to me. I remembered reading a newspaper article that said that animals could sense if you were feeling sad, lonely, or angry. None of the pets in the room seemed to be sensing my emotions, and it was better like this. I was used to being under the radar. I was used to being the third wheel. But this felt horrible! I had to stay in Luna's room all day because I knew that Dominik would be laying on the couch, a mountain of used tissues beside him.

Luna was rarely home. She was usually found crying in the library, but I knew that today, she wouldn't be there. The Russells, more like Luna, had paid extra to get a proper funeral for Courtney. The funeral was today. And even though Courtney was Dominik's twin sister, he seemed to care more about the death of Evelyn Atherton, a girl he barely knew. The thought made me want to vomit.

I stared at the ceiling motionless. One could think I was dead. I'm starting to understand that you can find out a lot about a place by looking at it's ceiling. A ceiling can tell you if you're in an expensive private suite or a filthy public bathroom. They tell you a lot.

I distanced myself from reality as I closed my eyes, picturing what I had heard last night.

"I'm paying the Magistratus for a funeral for Courtney." Luna had shouted. "I know you had a crush on this Evelyn Atherton, but your sister died and your not spending one ounce of energy to mourn her!"

"It's not like she was ever nice to you!" Dominik had shouted. I heard shuffling and I knew that Dominik had stood. "Evelyn triggered something inside me, and now she's gone. Its like part of my existence went into space to float into nothingness. I loved her and deep down, she loved me back."

"You've never spoken of a girl that way!" yelled back Luna. "You never spoke of Whitney, of Louisa, of Claudia, of Scarlett in that way . . . You've never said you felt that way to any of them! Goodness, you've never told *me* you love me that much! And I'm your sister!"

I couldn't stand the way Luna yelled at Dominik, the way Dominik still mourned the death of Evelyn Atherton. Before Mortmeisis hit, Luna took me to meet all her friends. Jo, Liza, Oscar, and Bella were all amazing. Lauren Atherton was nice, too. I couldn't meet Cara because she was over at Darla Frost's plece. But even then, Evelyn wasn't the nicest. I remember flinching when I saw her beautiful face, knowing that Dominik preferred her over me.

I had no one to mourn, nothing to do. The Russells had no more money for cat food. Even Cassie had to skip meals sometimes. Like me. We would all die. We all had no more money left.

I looked around the room, in search for an exit that wouldn't cross Dominik's path. There. My eyes landed on the air vent. I could pry it open and sneak outside. Luna would freak out if she got here and I wasn't here but I couldn't stay in this room any more.

I jumped onto the bed and as quietly as I could, pried the air vent open. It was easier than I thought it would be. Sterile air hit me, and I struggled to get myself up. Finally, I was in the air vent. I had to army crawl through the vent. Off in the distance, I heard a sign of civilization, the depressing noises making me want to turn back. I heard people weeping in the hallways. I crawled a bit more and soon heard a flushing toilet. I looked down through the vent. Perfect. I would land near the sinks in the Southern Public Bathroom. I pried the door open and jumped down, making a racket as I landed on the floor. I looked around. Thankfully, I was the only person in the bathroom at the time. I ran out of the door, not bothering to close the vent door behind me. As I did so, I hit something hard, a wall maybe. And everything went black.

Esme Hall

"Will she be alright, Dr. Poole?" I asked, frantically brushing my black hair out of my face. Like me, the girl laying on the bed also had black hair, but hers was curly. Mine was as straight as a pencil.

"Hard to say, Ms. Hall." answered Dr. Poole as he took his mask off, checking the monitor one last time. "You hit her really hard."

I covered my mouth, once again remembering how I had wanted to go to the restroom, and instead had hit a girl running at me. The girl had fallen to the ground, unconscious, the left side of her head bleeding from the impact. My brother squeezed my hand, next to me. I looked at him, desperately trying to find comfort, instead finding cold, purple eyes staring at me. I looked away.

"Dr. Poole, you must understand. Do whatever you can, to get this girl functioning properly," said my brother in a voice as hard as steel.

"Mr. Hall, I do not believe she is a cyborg." said the nurse.

Right. Cyborgs. Part human, part machine, part robot.

"Or a droid."

Droids. Robots. Same thing.

"She's human."

"Fix her, quickly. My sister and I must get going."

"Then get going, Mr. Hall! Someone has to pay her medical bills, and that person must be your sister. She hurt her!" yelled the doctor, making the girl stir. "Just because you're orphans, doesn't mean you won't pay for this! According to all our research, this girl is unknown. We have no contacts for her! And I do not think Parson's Orphanage would like to pay for this girl's injuries!"

Dr. Poole was right, of course. Parson's Orphanage was not going to pay for this. And we had no money. I would have to give up something. My hand instinctively reached toward the locket resting against my collarbone. The metal suddenly felt very cold and heavy. My brother,

Oliver didn't look at me. The locket was the most expensive thing I owned. It was the only thing left from the fire. My eyes teared up and there I was, a ten-year old girl, screaming in my bedroom for help.

Flames licked the carpet and the curtains. The smell of smoke and burning flesh burned my eyes, throat, and nose. Somewhere, far away, I heard Oliver screaming. But I couldn't go help him. I was trapped in my room. In hell. The fires danced around me as if happy to see my despair. The flames circled around me, grabbing at my ankles and wrists. I tried to escape, but it was no use. Suddenly the door burst open, and a masked figure came in, picking my limp body up and running outside.

The cool air slapped me in the face, sending a surge of shock down my spine. The firefighter set me down. Behind me, what was left of our mansion gleamed with flames. I wanted to cry for all I had lost. My beautiful room, the grand kitchen bustling with busy servants, my mom's office with overflowing piles of paperwork.

I noticed a trembling figure beside me, and with a jolt realized that this was Oliver. What was left of Oliver. One of his legs was badly burned, revealing burnt flesh. He winced in pain as he tried to move. I reached out to grab his hand but I stopped myself once I saw reality. A deep, bloody cut was inscribed into my right arm, the jagged line reaching from my wrist to my elbow. The cut itself was bloody and oozing but within it you could see a rugged landscape of charred flesh.

A cool mist spread over me like a blanket, at once eliminating any scent of smoke. The firefighters sprayed the mansion with foam for what seemed like hours. Finally, they stopped, letting me have an exclusive view of the remnants of our house. Everything was black, burned, and smoking.

Oliver was silently weeping beside me, and I spun around to see what he was crying at. The remnants of our parent's bodies were carried into one of the ambulances that came to help. Everything was burned black like charcoal. This all happened during one of the Sun's last eruptions.

After days of investigation, the only thing that had survived the fire had been found, and it was my mother's locket in a burnt jewelry box.

"Esme! Esme!" yelled Oliver as he frantically waved his hand over my face. The vision stopped and once again, I was in the cold, sterile room. "We need to go back to the orphanage."

I nodded. I looked at the girl's body, on the bed. She looked so pale, yet so beautiful. I turned to walk away but something caught my eye. A large purple ring on the inside of the girl's wrist.

Mortemisis.

Oliver Hall

"Dr. Poole, Dr. Poole!" screamed Esme, as she lurched away from the girl.

"What, Ms. Hall?" asked the doctor, obviously annoyed.

"The girl. Mortemisis!" screamed Esme.

Dr. Poole furrowed his brow, quickly put on his mask, and came over to the girl. Now that the doctor was inspecting her arm, I noticed a large purple ring on the inside of her wrist. Esme was right. Mortemisis.

"How old are you guys?" asked Dr. Poole.

"Fourteen," I answered, automatically.

"Fraternal twins, right?"

"Yes," whispered Esme. I turned to look at her.

We were the same, just different genders. Midnight black hair, in Esme's case, straight, purple eyes, and pale skin. Some people referred to us as "The Vampires". It was utter nonsense.

"Go, now. You are most vulnerable. Go, before you catch it!" yelled Dr. Poole. I grabbed Esme's hand, and yanked the door open, slamming it behind us. We ran through the Normalem sectors. We ran and ran. The figure of a beautiful girl appeared before me, and I stopped for fear of crashing into her. Esme crashed on the floor with a *thud*. The beautiful girl, scowled and ran over to help Esme up. She was not mourning someone, that was for sure.

The girl had golden blonde hair, soft blue eyes. Nothing about her was ordinary.

"Are you okay?" asked the beautiful girl, with a voice as clear as a bell. "Are you hurt?"

"I'm fine," said Esme, as she stood up, her voice just like the beautiful girl's. The two girls stared at each other and then laughed, both voices sending shrilly vibrations down my spine.

"I'm Bella Atherton," said the girl. "You are?"

"Esme Hall." said Esme. Bella beamed then looked at me. Our eyes locked for a moment, then she looked down and blushed. "This is Oliver. My brother."

"Are you twins?"

"Yep."

"Wow! Two of my older sisters are twins."

"Cool."

Bella and Esme talked for a while. I didn't pay attention to most of it. I was too mesmerized by Bella's eyes to care, but one sentence caught my attention.

"We're orphans."

Bella's eyes suddenly turned sad.

"We're orphans, too." said Bella.

"I'm so sorry." whispered Esme.

"But you're not at Parson's Orphanage. It's the only orphanage on the Super Astra."

Bella smiled.

"My oldest sister is nineteen, a legal adult. We're allowed to stay with her," explained Bella.

"Oh, that's nice," beamed Esme. I admired her for that enthusiasm. How could she be so happy when we just left a girl at the hospital to die?

"You know, I heard Parson's Orphanage is really bad. Maybe you can come over and stay with us."

"That would be nice!"

As much as I wanted to stay at Bella's, I knew that Mrs. Parson and Mr. Parson would never let us out. They made it quite clear when we came to the orphanage that we would stay there until we turn eighteen. Yet, the idea of us staying at Bella Atherton's house was absurd. We just met her. I pulled Esme aside, ignoring Bella's curious eyes as they plunged deep into my soul.

"Esme, we just met her. How can you be so happy when we're about to go back to the orphanage and when we were just forced to leave a dying girl in the hospital?" I asked harshly. Esme's eyes lowered, her expression darkened, and sadness filled her eyes. She looked like a bird, trapped in a cage for life. Technically, she was.

"I've never had a friend in my life. No one except Samantha West, and she abandoned me when we came to the orphanage. She was only my friend because our family had money. Bella looks friendly. She's an orphan, too, and she doesn't judge me. We understand each other. You like her, too. I can tell. Please, just let me be, Oliver. This could be my only chance to get a friend," pleaded Esme.

I looked at Esme. She was right, of course. Esme had never had a friend once she came to the orphanage. Everyone left her. She was alone. My friends left me, too. I made some friends in the orphanage, but none were really that close. Esme was the only person I had. Esme looked at me, and the feeling of sadness spread over me like a soft blanket. Esme had me, and only me. She needed more.

"Fine, but be careful, Esme. She could be anyone." I warned.

"Don't worry so much, Oliver. You want me to be friends with her, too."

Esme was right, of course. I smirked at her, and she beamed a hundred-dollar smile. Then, she ran to Bella, who smiled in return.

"So how old are you?" asked Esme. "I'm fourteen."

"Wow, me too." said Bella. "You know, we could probably go to my house, if you want. I know the orphanage is a bad place to be."

"Are you guys not mourning someone?" asked Esme.

Bella's face darkened.

"In fact, we are. Cara wouldn't be at the house anyway, though. Lauren is at the day-research center thing, so I'm all alone. Lauren won't be back 'till seven o'clock. And yet, I think you could stay in my room."

"But you aren't at an academy. It's still academy hours." said Esme.

"We don't have enough money for me to go to an academy."

"Oh. We have classes at the orphanage. Seven to two." said Esme.

"Who are you mourning?" I asked, just out of curiosity. Bella's face darkened again, and I immediately regretted my question.

"My mother and my sister." said Bella.

"But you don't look like you're mourning." noted Esme.

"Right. During the Third World War, I got sent away to Iceland to live with my Aunt Malena. My mother and my sisters never visited, so really, I wasn't that close to them. Their deaths still hurt, but the pain wore off some time ago." answered Bella.

"Oh," Esme and I said at the same time.

"So, do you want to come over?"

I hesitantly looked at Esme. Then I looked at my excuse the time. Five o'clock. We were late. We had to be at the orphanage at four thirty. We would get time-outs. Then, Murphy, Mr. and Mrs. Parson's bratty son would take a hold of me, and that was never fun. Once, he put a scorpion in my bed when I didn't come to the orphanage in time. Esme on the other hand, will get humiliated by the girls again. Juniper, Mr. and Mrs. Parson's daughter was the key to rumors. Juniper could say any absurd thing she wanted and all the kids in the orphanage believed it. She had a squad thing that followed her around no matter where she went. They were like her little servants.

Esme would get humiliated by Juniper, and I would get beat up or something by Murphy. We needed to go, now.

"Esme, we have to go. It's five o'clock."

The radiant smile vanished from Esme's pale face, and her face turned paler, if that was possible.

"I'm so sorry, Bella. But we have to go. I would love to stay in contact though?"

"Absolutely! Here are my coordinates. You can contact me any time!" said Bella as she wrote it on the inside of Esme's wrist in small numbers. Smart girl. Mr. Parson would beat us if he found the phone number. Juniper would ceaselessly humiliate Esme for having "a boy's phone number on her arm". And I would get beat up by Murphy for letting Esme out of my sight. Bella nodded once, and disappeared down the hallway.

"Let's go,"

Esme and I sprinted down a maze of Normalem corridors. Maybe, we could sneak in through the air vent. Unless Juniper was out for a walk.

Just our luck. In front of the door leading to the Parson's Orphanage main hall, a figure perfect enough to be a model in Milano, Italy stood. When she saw us she smiled an evil smile full of malice. Juniper. Her short red hair bounced against the sides of her face. She wore a creamy white gown made of satin. As if she was going to prom. She actually could have. She was seventeen.

Juniper had developed extreme curves over the years that made the guys at the orphanage swoon over her and her mesmerizing perfume every time she walked by. You had to admit, Juniper had exceptional beauty, but I wasn't attracted by it. I knew what kind of ugly thing lay behind all that beauty and makeup. An ugly soul.

"Ah, if it isn't my favorite orphan, Esme Hall. How are you? What's the matter? Cat got your tongue?" Juniper laughed at her own insult joke thing.

"If it isn't my least favorite Parson." I retorted. Juniper scowled, but schooled her expression quickly.

"Been waiting for you, Hall. Why are you late? Were you busy?" taunted Juniper, wiggling her eyebrows at the last part.

Esme scowled, and shook her head with disgust.

"What do you want, Juniper?" she asked.

"What don't I want?" she asked, circling around Esme, like a wolf circling around its prey.

"Juniper--"

"My father wants to see you, Hall," she said, violently grabbing Esme by the shoulder, and shoving her to the door. "You too, Smarts."

Juniper shoved me toward the door.

"Let's go, children. My father wants to show you some discipline."

Bella Atherton

I walked down the hallway, taking the longest route home. I didn't want to go home. Though no one was in the house, the gloomy feeling still lasted. I wandered the endless corridors, thinking about Esme and her twin brother Oliver. Esme was such a sweetheart. I didn't know what had led her to being an orphan, but I knew the story was heartbreaking. I had heard of the Hall story but, I didn't know exactly how it went.

Oliver on the other hand, was very stern. He kind of had to watch over Esme, as if she was younger than he was, which was not true. But something in Oliver caught my attention. He had this mystic appearance, very mysterious. He was cute, but I didn't have a crush on him. But the way, he looked at me, everytime our eyes met, made me uncomfortable. As if I was a prize that he *needed* to win. I wasn't a prize. I was a person. With feelings.

A loud siren, pierced the eerily silent air, making me jump.

"All passengers to their apartments. This is not a drill. This is an emergency. All passengers to their apartments!"

The message sent a shrill of fear down my spine. The message itself had no secret meaning. But it obviously had something to do with Mortemisis. I was tempted to stay where I was, to investigate what was happening. I couldn't just stay at the apartment and be a good girl. Lauren probably wouldn't notice my absence. She didn't notice anyone anymore.

I started down the corridor. Maybe Luna or Liza would be willing to help. Possibly Jo. Oscar was still too numb with pain. I turned the corner, to see a mob of weeping people. My hope vanished as I saw the sadness everyone carried. The sadness that I was unable to carry because of my past. Luna, Liza, and Jo would all be the same. Why did I think that maybe they would be fine? They've lived with their loved ones all their life. I, on the other hand, lived with Aunt Malena all my life. Then, Aunt Malena died of a stroke and I had to hide from the orphanage agencies to avoid getting into an orphanage. I'd only done that for two years. Then, the Sun went out.

I turned back, eager to get away from the mob. I would go to the apartment to get some supplies. If I would be out all night, I would need some Nutri and a night vision glasses to watch if the Magistratus would come for their nightly patrol.

After sprinting through a maze of corridors, I reached the apartment. I turned the knob and ran inside, gathering my Nutri and the night vision glasses. I wasn't in the house for more than three minutes before I ran out again.

It was hard to run through the hallway, without dropping my food. I managed, before a boy bumped into me. Ever so slightly, but everything I carried fell to the ground. I stumbled to find my footing, as my balance had been disrupted.

"Oh, I'm so sorry, Miss!" exclaimed the boy. I landed on the ground, hitting my head hard on the cold, tile floor.

The boy had platinum blond hair, combed to the side of his head. He wore black clothes. The boy had a pale face, and when he touched me to help me get up, his hands burned through my skin with coldness. It was as if I had touched an iceberg. The boy had dusty grey eyes, that mesmerized me in a way I did not want to be mesmerized.

"I'm so sorry, Miss," I stared at him, dumbfounded. He cleared his throat and straightened up. "Samuel Grey. But you can call me Sam, you know."

I stared at him for a few more moments, then schooled my own expression.

"Bella Atherton."

"Pleased to meet you, Bella. I'm so sorry about this," said Sam, as he started picking up my things from off the ground. I stared at him, like the idiot I was. "Should I take you to the doctor? Crap, everyone's going home! Uh, Bella, would you like me to escort you home?"

Our eyes met, but I looked away too soon, blushing furiously. When I finally looked up, his pale face was pink.

"Thank you, Sam, but I wasn't going home."

Right after I said this, I realized my mistake. He could be anyone. Anyone in the world. I covered my mouth with my hand and looked away.

"Where?"

"Huh?"

"Where were you going?"

"I . . . I can't tell you." I whispered.

"C'mon, you can trust me."

"No. How can I be sure that you won't rat me out to the Magistratus?"

Sam scowled.

"Were you going to steal something?"

"No! No! Not at all! I was going to visit my Aunt M--Sadie!" I lied.

"Your Aunt Msadie?"

"Yes!"

Sam scowled once more. Then his expression straightened.

"You're lying," he said.

"Y--no." I whispered.

"Tell me, sunshine."

I stood, frozen where I was. Sunshine. Something that I would possibly never see.

"Please, I'm going to help you, Bella."

"You don't know me."

"You're right, I don't. But I can *get* to know you."

"I'm going to find out why they want us in our apartments."

Right when I said it, I covered my mouth and looked away, again. Why was I so stupid?

"Mind if I come along?"

The question startled me. I thought he would surely rat me out to the Magistratus. I scowled at him, wondering how he could be so positive or whatever when he was most likely mourning a loved one. As if reading my mind, Sam answered my question.

"No, sunshine, I'm not mourning anyone."

"Anyone?"

"Anyone. Let's go. Before the Magistratus catch us dawdling."

We started through the corridors, Sam grinning like an idiot at everything I said. It annoyed me ever so slightly, but I thought it was cute. When I would ask him questions, though, he would scowl and ask me a question instead. As if he was a secretive person in need of keeping secrets. These days, everyone knew everything about everybody. It was as if neon signs glowed over our heads saying, *Hey! This is Bella Atherton's deepest secret!*

What was weird, though, was that I didn't see a sign over Sam's head spilling his secrets to the world. I saw a blank page.

"Now, sunshine, where are we going?"

Sam's new name for me startled me.

"Why do you call me 'sunshine'?" I asked, as I stayed away from him.

"Why not? Your hair is so bright and pretty, it reminds me of what used to be the Sun," answered Sam, grinning at me like an idiot.

Right. The Sun. What used to be of the Sun.

I looked away, my face feeling hot as I blushed. After my little presentation, I took a deep breath and faced him.

"Do you know where the Mortemisis Quarantines are?"

"Nope."

"Huh. What about where the control center is?" I asked hopefully.

"Are we going to fly this ship?" asked Sam. "No, sunshine, I don't know where it is. It's kept a secret from the public."

"Okay, very helpful. Do you know where the Imperium Council meetings are held?"

"Sunshine, how many times do I have to tell you. *No.* I'm just an average Imperium citizen."

"You're not average. You're not mourning someone." I pointed out. The name 'sunshine' was kind of hard to get used to but I knew no matter what I told him, he would never give up on that name. He was like a leech, clinging to my skin everywhere I went.

“Neither are you, sunshine.”

“True,”

“So, where do we go now?”

“We could eavesdrop on a Council meeting.”

“That’s illegal,”

“Not if we have an authorized pass. And I think I know just the person who would grant us that.” I said, smiling a mischievous grin.

Oscar Smith

Knock! Ugh. Who would want to come over when 95% of the citizens in Imperium were mourning and when the government just called for an emergency? I opened the door, and what I saw was not what I was expecting. Instead of a Magistratus officer, Bella Atherton and strange guy stood in the doorway. Who is he and what're they doing here?

"Hi Oscar!" beamed Bella. It made me sick to think that she lost her mother *and* her older sister, and she wasn't mourning anyone. I had lost three people.

Gabrielle had died of Mortemisis. Alexander had died of a painkiller overdose. Before his untimely death, I asked him why he was taking them. He said, *To numb the pain of mom's death.* Stupid nonsense. The next day, he died. Then, there was my mother's death. Her death was the most traumatic. She'd gone to the restroom at work, and they'd found her shriveled up and purple on the floor. The disease had been mutating, killing people in mere hours rather than days. Mom had gone to work, and she'd never came back.

When the Magistratus came back with her shriveled, purple body on a stretcher, I felt as if my world was ending. Every part of the sense in my existence faded. Every part except one. I kept thinking of Luna. I would tell myself that she was going through the same thing, too, though she wasn't mourning three people at once, she was still in a tough state. Maybe, I could get out of depression's abyss. Maybe I could help her on my way out.

The thought stirred something in me. If dad died as well, I would be sent to Parson's Orphanage, which to my knowledge, was living hell. If I died though, dad would surely kill himself.

"Bella, why are you here. You're supposed to be at your apartment. Don't you know that Lauren will be worried sick?" I was surprised when my voice came out like a frog's croak.

"In fact, Lauren barely notices me these days. She'll be fine."

"What's happened to you? You're not the Bella I remember. How can you be so selfish? Lauren does notice you, its just you don't notice her noticing you!"

"Nonsense, Oscar. We need to speak with your mother."

The last word of Bella's sentence made all my hope crumble.

"No," was all I managed to croak out.

"What? Oscar?" snapped Bella. She was so not the caring Bella I remembered from my childhood. This was a new Bella. This Bella was a selfish jerk that didn't care about other people's feelings. The guy next to Bella stirred and I realized I had forgotten he was there.

"Who is *he*?"

Once I said my words, I realized they sounded like daggers coated with poison.

"Sam Grey. Nice to meet you." said the guy, obviously uncomfortable by my grief.

"Bella Atherton. Take you and your boyfriend out of here. Before. It's. Too. Late." I threatened.

"No Oscar. I realize that you're in the process of mourning Gabrielle, but I really need to speak to your mother." said Bella.

"She's not here." I whispered.

"What do you mean? Is she at work? I thought Wednesday's were her days off."

"No."

"What do you mean by 'no'? Did they change her schedule?"

"No, Bella. Grow up and face reality."

With a jolt, I realized that Bella and I sounded just like when Evelyn was telling me about her mother's death. I suddenly knew how Evelyn felt like, being constantly asked uncomfortable questions that triggered avalanches of mixed emotions. But I also knew how Bella felt like. She actually did care. That's why she was asking so many questions. She wanted to know what was happening. But she didn't want to face the fact that maybe my mother had died of Mortemisis. Just like it didn't come to me that maybe after so many months of fighting Pollution Cancer, Aunt Leila just didn't have enough strength to cope with the disease anymore.

I turned to look at Bella. So many died each day, the Magistratus didn't bother to announce the deaths anymore. There was no way she could've heard about it. Poor Bella. She'd never been visited when she was in Iceland. I visited her once, but that was it. She only had her Aunt Malena, and when she'd died, Bella had been forced to grow up too fast. I realized that maybe Bella was more mature than me. Bella didn't want to go to an orphanage, so she hid. She worked jobs to pay her school and bills. She acted as an adult even though she was only fourteen, and maybe, just maybe that hardened her instincts to mourn.

I remember her briefly mourning Evelyn and her mother's death but that was it. In Iceland, she didn't even have enough time to mourn her Aunt Malena. I know her school was from seven to three. Afterwards, she would work a part-time job until nine o'clock. She'd stay up late to do her homework, and when she couldn't finish it, she would wake up early in the morning to finish it. Bella was more mature than I would've ever given her credit for. She'd suffered more hardships than I had. She had more experience in life than I had. She had more of everything.

"Bella, my mother died."

Bella's face turned pale, but that was her only reaction.

"I'm so sorry." she whispered. "I'll let you be."

Bella turned and walked down the corridor, tugging Sam behind her. I didn't have enough reaction time. Before I went out to look for Bella, she'd disappear into nothingness, along with her new boyfriend. With a jolt I realized maybe Bella wasn't the selfish one. Maybe I was.

Luna Russell

I sat on the edge of my bed, waiting for Nova to return. I still had no idea who she was but I believed she couldn't be Tiffany Ciapponi. And even if she was, she was innocent.

Nova's note still haunted me. She would be back. She would be careful. She had to take care of business. Sure, but she'd been gone for hours. And I didn't know how early in the morning she'd left. I had been at Courtney's funeral.

Her funeral had been short, because so many other people still paid extra to get proper funerals for their loved ones. The Athertons had paid for Evelyn's funeral, and the Kings had paid for Dayonara's funeral. I knew that the Sparks family desperately wanted a funeral for Kian, but they couldn't afford it. After all, the apartments on the Super Astra weren't free. We'd have to move into a Normalem apartment soon if we couldn't get enough money because trust me, working part-time at Geo-Research Center didn't get us enough money. Dominik didn't work at all, as he fell deeper into depression. I felt bad for him but he pushed away my every effort to help him. I couldn't do anything without triggering a tsunami of emotions.

Food was a problem. Nearly all my earnings went to paying this apartment. We barely had enough food for ourselves, and Dominik only ate during breakfast.

Crash! The sound startled me. All the pets were in my room and Dominik was usually very quiet unless we started arguing. Something must've happened. I ran across the hall, past what used to be Courtney's room and into Dominik's room.

It was messier than I remembered. His clothes were strewn everywhere, along with bedsheets and curtains outlining holographic windows. A robot lay disassembled, the parts lying all over the room. Near the closet lay a metal chair, probably the thing that made the noise. But where was Dominik.

As my eyes scanned the closet, I saw a horrifying picture. A heavy duty rope was tied to the upped racks of the closet. The other end of the rope was tied in a noose. And in that noose, Dominik's head, his body hanging like a bag of potatoes. I shrieked a sound that sounded more like a hurt cat did it rather than human. I ran over to Dominik, taking the noose off his head, catching his heavy body, and slumping to the ground, tears choking me. Dominik wasn't breathing as I cried over him. What had he done? After weeks of depression, after weeks of pushing me away, he had sought an escape to his grief. I cried for what seemed like hours, and unlike other times, the thought that Dominik was gone did not settle in deep in my stomach. The words, *Dominik is gone*, did not become hollow. How could Dominik do this to himself? Do this to me?

I heard another crash, and I flinched away from the sound, remembering the sound of the metal hair crashing to the wood floor. Around seven Magistratus officers burst in, carrying weapons and Mortemisis prevention masks.

"Hands up or I'll shoot!" yelled one of the men. Two men grabbed me, shoving me away from Dominik's lifeless body. I crashed into the mirror making hundreds of thousands of pieces of glass shatter, covering my body with scratches. The scratches didn't hurt, though. I was still too numb from pain to notice them. The two men that shoved me away from Dominik, stood before me, weapons pointed to my temple. I wasn't intimidated, though. Everything had lost its meaning. But I knew that I should care. I had friends that would mourn my death. Jo, Liza, Bella, Nova, and Oscar. Oh, Oscar. How I needed to see his god-like face. How I needed his comfort.

Two more Magistratus officers protruded tablets to fill out e-forms from their coat pockets, making pictures of the crime scene. After they finished, the rest of the officers started investigating the crime scene, putting anything suspicious into plastic bags. An officer came to gather my fingerprints, probably checking if I'd touched anything near the body. Sure enough, they found my fingerprints on the rope and on Dominik's body.

The two officers guarding me, roughly took my hands, placing them behind my back. I could feel the handcuffs getting tighter and tighter but I could care less. I needed time to mourn Dominik. He'd been nothing but a jerk to me, but I still loved him dearly. I remembered Dominik's words from before we left Earth. *Why are you wailing like a police siren?* I'd been angry at his carelessness then, but my anger seemed silly now.

The two Magistratus officers guided me through the hallways, they eventually tied my handcuffs to a pole so that they could do investigations. I slumped against the wall, letting the cold, hostile tiles beneath my legs make my body numb with cold. I hadn't done anything to hurt Dominik. Surely they would come back, apologize for my inconvenience and let me be. Then all the money I had saved up for bills would go for Dominik's funeral. I would then move to a Normalem apartment, and continue my part-time work at Geo-Research Center. Once I had enough money to pay the bills, I would continue my education.

But then, the grey walls of the Magistratus headquarters dulled my hopes. Those were high hopes with high bets. Unless some evident sign of evidence popped up, proving my innocence, the Magistratus would just assume I murdered my brother, sentencing me to a death-sentence. And afterwards, my body would be thrown off the ship into the nothingness.

I didn't know if minutes, hours, or days had passed when finally, the two Magistratus officers came to me.

"Up!" they commanded in unison, forcing me to get up.

I got my first good look at them, once I got up. The first officer, the one on my left, had brown hair with brown eyes. He was slightly shorter than the other officer who had flaming red hair that made his head look like it was on fire, and green eyes. His red hair reminded me of Liza.

"Sir, what's happening?" I asked one of the officers. He smirked.

"I don't know, young lady. . . " he said, as he laughed. Then his face turned serious and he started yelling. "WHY DID YOU KILL DOMINIK RUSSELL?"

"But no! This is a misunderstanding! I didn't kill him!" I cried, pushing myself against the cold wall in an attempt to escape the officers wrath.

The officer calmed down and smirked once again.

"Quite right. You're free. You know the neighbors, they were quite disturbed by your wailing." mused the smirking officer.

So the neighbors had called the Magistratus on me. I shook my head with disgust. Idiotic people.

The second officer, the quiet one unbuckled my handcuffs. I didn't think they were this tight before, but once I was free, my wrists felt relief almost immediately. The first officer fiddled with a piece of paper, and for the first time since Courtney's death I was filled with a burning desire to know what it was. Curiosity.

"What's that?" I asked, as innocently as I could.

"A note, from Dominik Russell. A suicide note. Perhaps you should read it."

The officer handed me the note, smirking as he did so. I unfolded the tattered piece of paper, surprised to see Dominik's handwriting. Why was I surprised?

Dear World,

I'm sorry to have hurt anyone who would have cared to love Dominik Russell. Before we left Earth, I fell in love with a girl. But that turned out only to be a crush. I used her death as an excuse for my depression. I was sad that that girl had died but she wasn't the reason for my depression. I loved my parents so very much. My father had died when I was very young. I've never known what it's like to have a father to guide you. And then my mother died. I loved her a lot. But when she sacrificed herself for the sake of humanity, I couldn't take it. Then Courtney who I also loved dearly died, too. All my loved ones were dying.

There are some people I would like to address this letter to. Firstly, my baby sister- Luna.

Luna this is only for you and I do not wish another set of eyes to read it. Luna, I know I was a jerk. I know you probably thought I didn't love you, but all the pain I caused you was because I loved you too much. I loved you so much, that soon, I got jealous of the happy life you lived. The life I wanted to live, but couldn't. You may think these are pure lies, and if I were you, I would think so too after everything I'd done to you. Under the bed, you will find a green box with a skull sticker on top. Open it. Luna, I've been saving this money for years. It's enough to help you go to college. Use it wisely, as it is the only nice thing I have ever given you. Don't mourn me, I don't deserve to be mourned. Don't throw away your money on a funeral. I don't deserve it. Don't mourn me. Don't throw away your money on a funeral. Remember me if you want, but you might as well forget I existed. It's the best for both of us.

My friends- Edward, Jonathan, Trevor, and Charlie. Guys, you were always there beside me during my ups and even my downs. Jonathan, you introduced me to Sara, the girl I dated longest. Charlie, you introduced me to Louise, my first crush. Edward, you were my first friend in middle school, and you were nice to me, even though I was the new kid that didn't belong anywhere. I didn't deserve that. Trevor, you were the one who made me go to my first real party. All of you were nice to me, something I didn't really deserve.

But now, my message to the world. I loved my family more than anything and seeing them get killed one by one tore my heart in pieces. I want to apologize to the loved ones I hurt, but isn't death the better option compared to when I was alive? When I was stuck in an emotional abyss, unable to get out?

Now this is for the Magistratus. I killed myself. No one else killed me.

Thank you World, and goodbye.
P.S- Be sure to throw my body off the ship ASAP

-Dominik Russell
02/17/2101

The letter shocked me. Dominik loved me? And he was sorry? How could I believe that after years of torment? And he wanted me to forget his existence. He didn't want to be mourned, or to have a funeral. I couldn't do that, though. And he saved money up for my college expenses? That wasn't the Dominik I knew. I used to know. I looked at the Magistratus in shock. Now both officers smirked.

"You read everything, didn't you?" I asked them, shaking my head with disgust. The officers just raised their eyebrows and kept on being silent. "Can't you accept a dead man's last request?"

"An officer's job is to acknowledge every piece of evidence." answered Officer 1.

The officers kept smirking at me as if they knew something I didn't.

"You took the money, didn't you?" I asked them. The officers smiled, and I snarled back. "What wrong with you? How ill in the brain do you have to be to do that?"

"Oh no, sweet girl, we didn't take your money." answered Officer 2.

"But don't worry, beautiful, we'll take it sooner or later." added Officer 1. "You see, we did some research about you. You work a part-time job at Geo-Research Center. You make more money in a week than we do in two. The apartments aren't free, you know."

Officer 1 smiled and made the sign for money, rubbing his fingertips together.

"What do you want?" I growled, ready for a fight if it came to that.

"You want to leave? You need to pay," said Officer 2.

"Pay?" I asked in disbelief.

"Pay,"

I was about to make a run for it, when a booming voice echoed through the corridors.

"Wolfe! McKinney! Let the lady go!"

A figure stormed into the room. Their boss. The Magister. A Magister is the new-and-improved version of a Sheriff.

The Magister was bald and had cold black eyes that reminded me of the sky without the Sun. Wolfe or Officer 1 and McKinney or Officer 2 both stepped aside, obviously intimidated by the Magister. The Magister nodded once and escorted me back to my apartment.

"Sorry for that, Ms. Russell. I might advise you to move in with a friend who is willing to sign legal documents to adopt you. You are an orphan now, you know, with no family. Tomorrow at 2pm, two representatives from Parson's Orphanage will come pick you up if there is no application deposited for your adoption. Any questions?"

"No, sir." I answered.

"Very well,"

The Magister ordered for Dominik's body to be taken down. Officers put it in big black bag with a zipper and took it with them. They stormed off down the hallway, leaving me bewildered and puzzled. Who would want to take me in, when all my friends were mourning. Tomorrow morning, I would go around and ask.

I walked into the house, bothered by the silence. I didn't know what I was doing but I soon found myself at the table with a piece of paper and a pencil.

After writing the letter I felt compelled to hand it up in what used to be Dominik's room. I instantly felt better as if a heavy weight had been lifted from my frail shoulders. I would not mourn Dominik if that was his last request. I would start a new chapter.

Dear Dominik,

I trust that what you wrote was true, and I want you to know that I love you, too. Though, I will not mourn you like you requested, I will never forget you. Although you tormented me all my life, I'm glad you were in it. You made me stronger. I know you made your choices and though I would prefer you to be alive, I respect your choice. I hope you're in a better place now. Thank you for the money. I will use them for college purposes only. Know that I accept your apology for hurting me, but now it's my turn. I apologize for not being able to help you more. Though you pushed my every effort away, I should've tried harder, and maybe I wouldn't be writing this. I love you dearly, Dominik. Remember that. I will always look up to the stars, searching for you.

With love,
Luna

Liza King

I woke up with a start. The nightmare had been more than I wished for. I'd dreamed of Angelica and how we were walking along the beach. Suddenly, Angelica turned to me and said, "I was better off without you."

She became a cold mist, that circled me, like a cat stalking its prey. I screamed but the mist seemed to make my screams unhearable. Finally, the ground opened up, swallowing me and my desperate screams. Around me, Angelica's voice kept on saying, "I was better off without you."

As I fell, my mother's ghost came to me, holding out her hand, begging me to come to her.

"Little baby. Little Liza. Come to Momma." said my mother, in a voice so sweet and pretty, it sent shivers down my spine. This was not my mother's voice. It was not Dayonara King's voice. My mother like Angelica, turned into mist and encircled me, finally slaughtering my last efforts and suffocating me to death.

I turned the light on, begging for the nightmare to leave me once and for all. *Angelica wouldn't say such a thing*, I chided myself. The clock glared 3:49. I'd woken up early in the morning. So early, I knew I wouldn't be able to fall asleep again.

In the light, I studied myself. I looked exactly like before, and I was confused to why I thought I would look different. I had gotten over my mother's death. Though I missed my mother dearly, I knew that even if I mourned, she wouldn't be coming back. I knew what my mother would say if I was still mourning.

Oh Liza, get a hold of yourself! I gave life to you so that you could do great things in life! Don't waste precious time! Don't mourn me, child! Not now!

My amber eyes stared back at me and I noticed something unusual. I twisted my head to see what was on my neck. What I saw made me gasp, then shriek. On my neck was a small purple ring, glaring at me like an invitation to go through the Doors of Death. Mortemisis had struck again.

Jo Sparks

I was thinking how Kian's death had turned into a throbbing pain rather than a constant agonizing one. I wonder what Kian would do right now if he was still alive. He would probably be making out with Courtney Russell, or hanging out with his friends, Vladimir and Toby. How I wished he could be here. Though he never thought much of me, I knew he loved me. And although he teased me 24/7, I still loved him. Very much.

I heard the door burst open, and I wondered who it could be. Mom and dad were still very numb, even weeks after Kian's death they moved slowly around the house, like phantoms making the least amount of noise as possible. Because noise is what Kian always made.

Liza yelled my name so loudly, Luna must've heard it from the other side of the ship. I ran through the hallway door to see what was happening. I knew Liza had gotten over her mother's inevitable death but I never expected her to fly in like that.

Liza was panting, her amber eyes wide with panic. She was as white as snow. What was happening? I walked closer to Liza but she screamed at me to stay away.

"Stay away! You'll get sick!" she screamed.

"What . . . Liza, what's happening?" I asked, panicking as well. "Tell me. Now."

"Mortemisis," whispered Liza, as she edged away from me.

"Liza, tell me now. What's happening? I think you owe me an explanation after you burst through the door like that."

"Mortemisis. Jo, I got sick."

"Nonsense." I muttered in disbelief. Liza with Mortemisis? That couldn't be true.

"Jo, I'm not lying." whispered Liza. She turned her head, showing me a small purple ring with three other rings surrounding it. The sight made my insides quiver. The purple blotch glared at me, tearing me apart, piece by piece. It was as if Death had touched Liza. My eyes widened and

I looked away. How could Liza join the billions killed? How could Liza die in just a few hours, leaving me hopeless once again. She just couldn't die. "I have Mortemisis."

"No," I whispered, a savage monster tearing up everything I had been trying to build after Kian's death. "How could this be? When have you been out of the apartment?"

"I went out on a stroll yesterday afternoon. Otherwise, I haven't been anywhere." said Liza, touching the rings on her neck as if they would magically disappear. I would do anything to see that happen. "I'm so sorry, Jo. I really am. I don't want to leave you like this. You just recovered after Kian's death."

Liza started sobbing, collapsing on the floor. I ran over to her, hugging my arms protectively around her now frail body. Mortemisis microbes were now eating away at every tissue, muscle, joint, and bone this beautiful body held.

"Stop, Jo!" shrieked Liza. "I'll get you sick!"

"I rather die with you than let you die alone." I said, taking Liza's hands while meeting her eyes. "You are not dying alone. Do you hear me?"

"No! Think of what your parents would do if you died, Jo!"

"My parents barely notice my presence. They'll get over my death quickly."

"Jo! Your parents love and tell you what? They'll kill themselves without you holding the shattered pieces of their hearts together."

"Then we'll be one happy family in heaven."

"No!"

"Please Liza-"

"No! You'll get over me! We've only been dating for a year! You'll find a new girlfriend. You'll graduate from science institute and find a cure to Mortemisis. Then you'll get married . . . start a . . . family. . . and be happy." said Liza as she sobbed on the floor.

"No, Liza. You're the only one I could ever love."

"I'm your first girlfriend! How can you say that when you've never tried to be happy with someone else?"

"I didn't want a second try because I got lucky the first," I said, embracing Liza.

"Nonsense," mumbled Liza. "You'll get over me, you'll fall in love with someone else."

"No. Liza Natalie King! I look at you and see the rest of my life in front of my eyes. There is no other one."

Liza looked at me, her face full of innocence, desperation, and panic. Suddenly, we were on the floor, kissing. The kiss was short but passionate, our hearts poured into that one kiss.

"I shouldn't have done that. You'll get sick." grumbled Liza, as she got up from the floor and ran away, leaving me blank-minded.

My mind was still processing the kiss. It was more than I could've asked for, but when I snapped out of the shock, I realized that Liza wasn't in the apartment. I hadn't heard where she was going to go. She would eventually be at the hospital, but I couldn't wait until eventually. I needed to know where she was. And I needed to know *now*.

Esme Hall

Juniper dragged us through the hallway, muttering words full of malice.

"Oh, father will show the Halls that the world doesn't revolve around them. It revolves around me. Maybe he'll tie them up to a metal pole and whip them. How funny it would be if dad put the pole in a freezing chamber, and then made the Halls lick the pole. It would look as if they're kissing and their tongues got tied up! Hahahaha!"

Oliver nudged me and smirked. He was right. Juniper was simply going mad with malice. I adjusted my position so that Juniper's nails weren't digging into my shoulder blade as much. We were nearly to Mr. Parson's office and I could hear his deep voice.

"No Rosalie, we have enough room for all three-hundred orphans." said Mr. Parson. I could tell he was getting irritated with Mrs. Parson. Mrs. Parson's squeaky little excuse for a voice rang in my ears.

"But the Magister informed me that another child could be coming to the orphanage. A Russell, in fact. Did you know that the child's family died out, the mother stayed on Earth, the father died in World War Three and both its siblings died of Mortemisis."

"Ugh, why are you telling me this, Rosalie? And why did I ever open an orphanage?"

"You love kids." chimed Mrs . Parson.

Juniper lead us through the door, and dread quickly settled into my stomach. In the far end of the room, a large hammer glistened on the wall. Mr. Parson always said he used it on naughty children but he never once used it on us so, I suspected he was bluffing. A large persian rug was under our feet, no longer soft after decades of being stepped on. Paintings of Mr. Parson's family outlined the room. Before us was a large desk, covered with several skyscrapers of papers, documents, bills, and more. Mr. Parson, a large, burly man with a handsome mustache sat there. Like always, he wore a green suit with a fake violet tucked in the chest pocket. He was bald and had muddy brown eyes.

Next to him, was a tall and skinny woman with flaming red hair, pulled back into a bun, and stunning blue eyes. Everything about her was copy-pasted on Juniper. And everything, except the baldness, about Mr. Parson was duplicated into Murphy. It was as if the family was made of two originals and two clones. Mrs. Parson reminded me of a toothpick, dipped in red paint. She was so skinny, always on a harsh diet. She had a crooked nose and small lips almost always in a frown.

When Mr. Parson saw our arrival, he smiled a smile that only villains in cartoons could smile. Mrs. Parson frowned and went over to investigate Sir Edward Parson's portrait.

"Oh yes, I *love* children," said Mr. Parson. "Juniper, tell me everything."

Juniper smirked.

"Esme and Oliver Hall came back to the orphanage at five o'clock rather than at four thirty. *And* Esme has a number, written on the inside of her wrist." announced Juniper, smirking when she saw my reaction. How did Juniper see Bella's number? It was on the inside of my *wrist*. It's not like I waved my hand around in front of her. "Yes Esme. I did see your little secret. Was it a boy? Rescuing you from the paradise orphanage my father built from scratch?"

"Wait, why would she need rescuing if this was a paradise orphanage?" asked Oliver, as he turned to look at Juniper. I stood there for a moment? What was Oliver trying to do? The idea blazed in my head like a wildfire. Oliver was buying me time so I could erase Bella's number. I looked at her number, memorizing all the numbers. I had a photographic memory so, memorizing the number wouldn't be hard. I licked my finger and hid my hands behind my back. Soon, all the evidence of Bella's number was gone. Not even a mark. I was proud of myself.

"Stop bickering about nonsense!" yelled Mr. Parson, as he grabbed Oliver's collar, throwing Oliver to the floor. He then came from behind his desk, embracing Juniper as if she was a hero or something. I ran over to

Oliver, supporting his head, for it was obvious he had hit it against the desk. Oliver didn't look stunned, though. He grabbed my wrist, looking for any trace of the number. When he found nothing, he smiled and gently hoisted himself up. Mr. Parson was still hugging Juniper.

"Oliver, are you okay?" I asked, as Oliver rubbed the back of his head.

"Yeah, I'm fine."

"Ms. Hall, come here." ordered Mr. Parson's deep voice. I turned around, just in time to see Juniper flashing me a large grin full of malice. "Show me your arm."

I confidently showed him my arm, knowing that no trace of the phone number still existed. He would never know. Mr. Parson took my arm violently, turning it at all angles, some painful others not. Mr. Parson never found a trace of a phone number. He scowled and his brows furrowed. He was obviously frustrated with himself.

"Juniper, where's the supposed phone number you where blabbing about?" asked Mr. Parson, his voice stern, his eyes hard with rage. Oliver smirked at Juniper. I just smiled. Juniper would be proven wrong for once. "Where? Juniper Sienna Parson. Tell. Me. Where. Is. The. Supposed. Phone. Number. Did you really lie to me, to get the Halls in trouble? After everything I've done to ensure your comfort?"

For once, Mr. Parson looked disappointed in Juniper. Juniper turned away, her eyes glistening. She'd never been wrong. And her father had never been so disappointed in her. Mr. Parson looked at us, sympathy in his eyes, which was a first. But when Juniper looked back at us, Mr. Parson's face hardened. I realized that maybe he played this charade because his daughter was full of malice.

"Because you were late, you will be helping Ms. Estelle wash the dishes after tonight's dinner. Off you go!"

Oliver and I scurried through the hallway, straight to the dormitories. The brown carpet was beginning to grow mold in the corners, even though we've only been on the ship for less than seven months. The robomaids didn't do a good job, that was obvious. The beige wallpaper was starting to peel off in some places. The flickering lights above our heads threatened to give out, sending the hallway into complete darkness.

"That was good, Esme. I didn't think you would take the hint," mused Oliver, as he rubbed his head.

"Do you really think I'm that stupid, Oliver? Of course I would take your hint. I memorized the number, too."

"Did you see the look on Juniper's face?" asked Oliver, as he doubled over, laughing.

"Yeah." I said, lost in thought. "She'll be spreading awful rumors soon."

"No matter. You're strong. You can handle them because you know they're not true. But that look, though."

Oliver started laughing again. I sighed and started walking through the doorway leading to the Girl's Dormitory. I lingered in the doorway.

"Oliver, I'll go to Krystal. She'll have an ice-pack for you."

"Honestly Esme, stop fretting. I'm fine." said Oliver, turning away so I couldn't see him rub his head, once again.

"Nonsense," I muttered. "Wait for me here in ten minutes."

I walked through the doorway, desperate to find Krystal. Krystal was old enough to work a part-time job as a nurse at the hospital. She was seventeen, and like Juniper, was days from being eighteen. Krystal sometimes smuggled medical supplies into the orphanage. She was always open to helping the hurt. Krystal had to have an ice pack.

I found Krystal, studying on the couch, near the holographic fire. This was the common-room, where all the girls hung out in their free time. I walked over to Krystal and once she noticed me, her weary black eyes followed my every movement. Her black hair was pulled into a tight bun, making her exposed olive-skin look like gold under the flickering light of the fire. Krystal smiled, a weak thing that shouldn't even be counted as a smile.

"What did you hurt this time?" asked Krystal. She knew me well. I would come to her almost every week with cuts and sprains.

"Oh, it's not me this time," I said, flashing a persuasive grin. "It's Oliver. Mr. Parson threw him onto the ground and he banged his head on the desk. He banged it hard. He keeps on rubbing it and I suspect a concussion."

"Did he complain of a headache?"

"No, but you know Oliver. He never complains no matter how serious something may be. He didn't even complain when Murphy broke his arm three summers ago."

"Right. Did he have a temporary loss of consciousness?"

"No,"

"What about confusion?"

"No, not really."

"What about dizziness, or 'seeing stars'?" asked Krystal, scowling in concentration.

"Um, I don't think so."

"What about nausea?"

"I don't think so."

"Did he vomit?"

"No! Mr. Parson would kill him if he puked in his office!"

"Esme, I think he just hit his head really hard. I'll get you an ice pack," said Krystal, as she got up from the couch, heading over to the 14+ dormitories. I sat on the couch, looking at the holographic fire. It had the same color of real fire, or so they advertised. The holographic fire shed light but no warmth. You could stick your hand through it and you'll be fine.

Krystal soon came back, carrying a large ice pack in one hand, and pain medicine in the other. She greeted me with an apologetic smile, because if you knew Krystal, you knew that she would always give you more than you asked for.

"Sorry, but I think if Oliver is constantly rubbing his head, it must bother him. I think he should take this medicine."

I took the medicine and the ice pack from Krystal, giving her one of my signature smiles. Krystal was really caring and I didn't know what I would do if she wasn't here. I wouldn't know what I would do when she wasn't here. And that was just days away.

Krystal smiled at me, and just as I was turning away, saying "Thank you," she put her hand on my shoulder, stopping me.

"Esme, I know I can trust you." she started. "I don't think I can trust Simone and Nicole with this."

"What about your sisters Violette and Stefani?" I asked, curiosity growing inside me. Krystal, Stefani, and Violette were all triplets. More than one child at once was very common, so when the triplets came to the orphanage, no one was surprised. Their best friends, Simone and Nicole, were twins. I knew about seven pairs of twins at the orphanage: Carla and Daniela, Kira and Steven, Tomas and Micael, Albena and Nya, Klare and Martha, Adonis and Donovan, and Oliver and me.

I knew of three sets of triplets and a set of quadruplets.

"No," laughed Krystal, as she threw her hair back. "Violette and Stefani will be coming with me, once we turn eighteen. I need you to look after Fynn."

"Fynn?"

"Uh-huh." said Krystal, now looking uncomfortable. "Make sure he doesn't do anything stupid."

Fynn Chase.

Fynn was Krystal's boyfriend. He was only a few weeks younger than Krystal and her sisters, then again, she seemed so nervous. Sure, he did stupid things, like make fun of Juniper's snotty attitude, and pick fights with Murphy.

Fynn had dusty blond hair, brown eyes, and lots of courage. He would laugh and joke openly with all girls, which drove Nicole crazy when she was dating him. Their romance was short-lived. With Krystal, though, things are different. She doesn't care who he talks to as long as he doesn't cheat on her. She understands that he has full freedom to talk to whoever he wants, whenever he wants.

"And why me and not Simone or Nicole?" I asked, reluctantly.

"Nicole will be eighteen a day after me." explained Krystal, tapping her foot impatiently. "Simone is. . ."

"What?"

"She's running away from the orphanage," whispered Krystal. "If she gets caught, she'll be thrown off the ship for betraying Imperium."

Krystal started crying, and I reluctantly hugged her.

"That's why I need you, Esme. Please."

"Fine,"

I hugged Krystal once again and walked out of the common room, heading over to where I told Oliver to meet me. Unsurprisingly, Oliver was nowhere to be seen. I sighed. Why try to do something nice for him when he would just throw away my efforts? I sighed, once again, and walked back into the common room.

Oliver Hall

I felt dizzy as I walked into the boy's common room. I racked my brain to find some information. What had Esme said before she walked into the girl's common room?

No matter how much I searched, I was clueless to what Esme had said.

I sighed, and slumped down on the couch. Fynn walked over to me, grinning like the irresponsible idiot he was.

"Hey Olive!" he said, casually, as he sat down next to me.

"It's Oliver," I grumbled.

"What's wrong? You look sick."

"I feel dizzy, confused, and. . . did I say sick?."

Fynn raised his eyebrows in suspicion and looked at his WristPlay. Then called someone, but my mind was so fuzzy, I couldn't concentrate on who it was.

"Hey babe. Fynn here. No Krystie, I'm not in trouble. Oliver's here. He looks very bad. Yeah. We should meet at the Crosspoint."

Crosspoint. The place between the two dormitories.

"Let's go, Olive. We're gonna meet Krystal."

Fynn dragged me from the couch over to the Crosspoint. Did I look that bad that Fynn had to call Krystal?

I saw Krystal waiting for us. Her arms were crossed but she had a kind, forgiving look on her face. Next to her, though, was Esme. Esme looked annoyed. Why was she annoyed? What did I do?

"About time you came, Airhead," said Esme, as she shook her head. I smiled. Esme might be annoyed but she didn't hold grudges long. She would forgive me for not following her instructions.

Krystal came over to Fynn, telling him something about going to The Place. I didn't want to go to The Place, though. It was too far of a walk.

"I agree," said Esme, as she came closer to Krystal and Fynn. I wobbled a bit, forcing Esme to grab my wrist for support. "We'll get spotted by one of the Parsons. Or Ebony and her gang."

Ugh. I forced myself not to gag as I thought of Juniper and Ebony. Juniper was a rumor-spreading machine. We all knew that. But Ebony had taken us by surprise. She was the first crush I ever had. With those stunning pink-ish eyes, beautiful caramel brown hair, and contagious smile, Ebony had stolen my heart back when I was twelve. She'd been normal then. Afterwards, she'd started hanging out with Juniper and her little squad. Juniper was the rumor-spreading machine and Ebony Armstrong, Veronika Graves, Harmony Foster, Penny Lewis, and Jessika Herbert were her information resources. It was like Juniper was the body of the monstrous kraken and Ebony, Harmony, Veronika, Penny, and Jessika were all the tentacles, grabbing at every piece of information and hiding behind every corner.

"Let's go," urged Esme, pulling me along. I didn't want to go to the secret room we called The Place, though. I stumbled once, then twice, finally collapsing on the floor. I heard Esme scream, and Krystal calming her. I felt Fynn's strong hands picking my limp body up, and everything went black.

Liza King

I didn't want to go to the hospital. They wouldn't be able to save me anyways. I would just die and join all the other victims of Mortemisis. I would join my mother. But I would leave Jo, and unless he stopped following me through the corridors, yelling my name, he would join me, too. Jo had followed me and no matter how many times I circled the ship to escape him, he kept following me. Though my red hair probably wouldn't be hard to spot.

Not that I didn't want him by me. I *needed* to be by him, but I didn't want his death to be at my expense.

"Liza! Stop! Please!"

NO, I screamed in my head. Jo would not die with me.

"Liza! Stop running away from me! I have Mortemisis! There's nothing you can do about it now!"

I stopped in my tracks. Jo. Mortemisis. No solution. My brain processes the information in a painfully slow way. Jo had Mortemisis?

I reluctantly turned around. What if Jo just said that to stop me?

Jo came up to me breathless.

"How many times do you have to circle the ship before you get the message?" asked Jo.

"Not funny. You said you had Mortemisis."

"I do, though."

Jo pointed to his ankle. I hadn't realized he'd been following me *barefoot*.

I looked at his ankle, screaming when I saw the evidence of his appointment with Death. On his ankle was a medium-sized purple ring. The intense color of the purple glared at me. What had I done? I'd ruined his family and his life. Jo could've gone to science insitute. He would've married and had a family. He could've watched his kids grow up as he became a grandpa. He would retire and one day, he would die a peaceful death. Not a death caused by a pandemic.

I screamed again, but this time collapsed on the ground, the tears choking me.

"Liza!"

Jo was suddenly next to me, embracing me in his arms.

"What have I done?" I choked out.

"Liza, stop," said Jo, his voice stern. I stopped, looking into his large eyes. "I'm happy now. I want to die with you. And you will not spend your last hours crying over me."

I wiped my tears away.

"How do you want to spend your last hours?"

"Stop. Just give me a second."

I processed the information in silence, and came to the conclusion that like with my mother, no matter how hard I cried over him, the purple ring would not disappear.

"I want to be with you."

Jo seemed to like this. He grinned.

"Our interests are similar. I want to be with you, too."

We started walking mindlessly around the corridors. Jo's hand was at my waist pulling me closer and closer to him. I buried my face in his broad chest and soon Jo sat down, pulling me with him. I saw that we were on the covered balcony, where the only windows were. We were overlooking the stars.

I thought about what I had done, and what I would leave in this world. I would leave some heart-broken friends and family. But I would have Jo. Forever. Just like I always dreamed about. Jo shifted so that he was facing me, his thumb tracing my cheekbone.

As if reading my thoughts, he said, "Forever and ever."

His lips crashed into mine, and I wasn't afraid of hurting him this time. We were equal. My lips responded and soon, he was pushing me against his body, but my hands were unable to leave the railing. Finally, my hands gave up, sending us both on the floor. Jo must've realized that we were doing *this* in a public space. His lips faltered, and it was enough to tell me to stop.

I looked at him, sorry that the beautiful feeling was now over. I *needed* Jo and he needed me, too. We smiled at each other, as we stood there, watching the stars glide gently passed us. Jo winked at me as he reached for my hand, his trembling hand intertwined with mine. He guided us toward his apartment . . . but how distant everything seemed. . . how distant. I collapsed onto the floor, now on the rim of consciousness. I could feel my left hand twitching as Jo knelt next to me, his frail arms picking me up and guiding me into the apartment. How close I was. . . I was on the rim. . .

I woke up, happy to find Jo's arms tight around me. I felt tired and frail. I would have mere hours now, if even that. Jo must've woken up as well, for he turned to me. I gasped when I saw him covered in purple rings. He was now shriveled up and purple, and I guessed that I would only be worse. Jo, however, said "Hello, beautiful."

I shook my head and touched my face. It was like touching a dried fruit. Wrinkles were everywhere. I looked down to my purple hands and gasped. I turned around, greeted by the alarm clock. It read *12:03*. It was midnight.

A shock of electricity coursed through my body, making me scream. I had the sudden urge to lie down and fall asleep forever. Next to me, Jo hissed and grunted with pain, squeezing my frail body even tighter. I knew that these were our last minutes. I looked at Jo and knew that these were our last moments together. Our last minutes of life. Jo pulled me closer to him. His breath smelled sour.

We didn't say anything for a while, before I whispered, "Forever."
"Forever," agreed Jo. "And ever."
Jo pulled me closer and I shut my eyes for one last time.

Sam Grey

I walked down the covered balcony, thinking about Bella. I'd been at her house mere moments ago, but I left because right now, I wasn't welcomed. Bella was grieving over the death of Liza King and Jo Sparks. They had been found by Jo's parents, who had been shocked to find both Jo and Liza on the floor, both covered in purple rings. Both Liza and Jo had died. Unlike other deaths, this one found its way to the public. Something about a mutating line of microbes found on Jo Sparks' body. Both the parents of Liza and Jo were devastated and Felix Sparks, Jo's dad, had killed himself the day his son's body had been found. Everyone had to wear preventive masks now, for Mortemisis was everywhere.

I sighed as I straightened my mask. It was almost time to pick Evanna up from daycare. I pictured Evanna's soft platinum blonde curls as they bounced by her face when she jumped in my arms. She would have a large smile and her hazel eyes would be full of excitement and wonder.

If anyone had learned how to make money during Imperium's crisis, it was my mom and dad. My mom, Cyrene, had invented the idea of *Mortemisis Control* and *MoretmisisXXX*. My dad, Patrick, had followed along. They sold everything. From water bottles to masks, you name it. My parents had it all. And it all said that it could prevent Mortemisis for up to 24 hours, so you had to buy lots of a product at a time. It was a money-making machine. Whenever I asked my parents if the stuff actually works, my mother would just come, stroke my hair saying, *Hush! You need not know.*

I suspected them of fraud. They never told me, their *son*, if it works, so I guessed it just didn't work. But Imperium was desperate, and we were rich and according to my mother, everything was okay.

I walked into the daycare center, but instead of being greeted with wild shrieks and laughs of glee, I was greeted with an eerie silence. I wondered what was wrong as I ventured further into the center. I didn't see one kid in sight. I looked around, nervous. It looked as if someone had died.

I spotted a figure coming at me, and I recognized Ivory Hamilton. Ivory paused, looking nervous to see me. Her beautiful dirty-blonde hair gleamed in the harsh light of the lightbulbs hanging overhead. She had beautiful green eyes that only gleamed in amazement every time I spoke to her.

Ivory was my age, and she worked a part-time job at the daycare center as one of the child counselors. She knew a lot about psychology and always impressed me with her knowledge. Her older sister, Ever, had gotten Pollution Cancer when she was thirteen. Ever had died last year at the age of seventeen. The fight had been long. Very long. Very few people could fight Pollution Cancer for that long. After Ever had died, Ivory had started work here in hopes of helping her family escape the large debt they carried. The medications and therapies weren't free.

I looked at Ivory, her weary face concerning me.

Ivory mumbled something to herself, then she sped toward me.

"Sam, you shouldn't be here," she said, her voice quivering.

"Why? I came to pick up Evanna."

"Evanna . . ."

"What, Ivory? Tell me."

Ivory looked extremely nervous.

"Evanna got a strand of Mortemisis." she whispered.

I felt the color drain from my face.

"What?"

"She said a man in white offered her candy while she was walking to daycare with the maid. She said the candy tasted sour and an hour later she got her first ring." whispered Ivory. She held out her hand to comfort me but I didn't want her comfort at this very moment. I wanted to be left alone.

How could Evanna accept candy from a stranger? Sure, she walked to daycare everyday with Hope, the maid, because I helped my parents out with the business, but Evanna was smart. And how could Hope let her do that?

"Where is she?"

"Sam, calm down. Please."

"I don't need your counseling skills now, Ivory." I snapped. Ivory still looked nervous, but didn't flinch when I said that. "Where is she? I have a right to see my sister?"

"She's severly sick, Sam."

I shook my head. This was not right. How? HOW? How could this be?

I spun around, ignoring Ivory's requests. I would not come back. I needed to go to my parents. They would know what to do. Or would they?

The sprint through the ship was a daze. I vaguely remembered the doors and elevators whizzing past me. I knocked on the door of *Grey's Mortemisis Control*. Kate's soft voice told me to come in.

I walked in, Kate- the receptionist, greeting me with a warm smile. I, did not return the smile. Kate frowned and came over to me.

"What do you need, Sam?" she asked, as she crossed her arms.

"My parents. Where are they?" I asked.

"Mrs. Grey is in an executive meeting with Mrs. Christabelle Carey," answered Kate. "Mr. Grey is currently available. He's in his office."

I thanked Kate and ran over to the main office, it's glass doors leaning over me, like mythological giants. I opened the door, heading toward my dad's desk. He glanced up, momentarily, before his eyes trailed back to his laptop.

"What's up Slam Sam?"

My father's nickname annoyed me, but only slightly. I had more important things to think about and I wouldn't get too annoyed just because my father forgot I hadn't played basketball for the last six years.

"Evanna. . ."

"What about her?" said my father, just as he sipped some coffee.

"She got Mortemisis," I sputtered.

My father spit out his coffee as he jumped to his feet.

"Evanna. Got. Mortemisis?"

I barely managed to nod.

My dad ran past me, darting into the Executive Meeting Room. I ran after my dad.

My mom was situated on a chair, a bunch of papers and documents in front of her. Across from her sat Imperium's president, Christabelle Carey. She smiled at me, but it was obvious she was uncomfortable by our performance.

"Cyrene! Evanna! She's got Mortemisis!"

My mother jumped to her feet.

"What?"

"Cyrene, she's got Mortemisis!" yelled my father.

"What?" screamed my mother.

President Carey looked clam, a smug smile on her face.

"You were just telling me about your Motemisis cure," said President Carey, as she smoothed out her dress. "Let's see if it works."

"No!" my mother and father screamed at the same time.

"Cyrene, you said it works like a charm." prompted President Carey. "Why don't you want to cure your daughter?"

"Yes, but. . ."

"Ah Kevin, won't you tell me more about the cure?"

"President Carey, the cure. . ."

"Doesn't really work, right?" I asked, suspicion rolling in. My parents glared at me. President Carey smiled.

"The boy's right. Does the stuff work? Let's test it on your daughter?" said President Carey. "Or should I frame you for fraud?"

My father gulped while my mother stared at the floor. It was all a lie. Nothing was going to save Evanna. She was going to die.

And that's when I exploded.

Oscar Smith

I walked down the hallway to my apartment, expecting Luna. She'd moved in a couple days ago, after Dominik had died. I remembered how she came to the door all frail and tired but she was still beautiful. Still an angel. Still the girl that stole my heart many months ago. Luna had fallen on her knees and begged to move in. The decision wasn't hard to make. I wanted Luna beside me. My dad didn't care as he never came home from the pubs.

I twisted the brass knob, opening the door. The sound of peaceful music drifted through the air and the scent of bamboo and lily candles pleased my nose. The room was dark, the only light coming from the candles scattered all over the floor. In the middle was a figure, and I recognized Luna's frail, skinny figure.

I crept along the edges of the room, careful as not to disturb Luna. In my effort to keep Luna at peace, one of the candles grabbed at my pants, setting them on fire.

"Crap!" I yelled, clamping my mouth shut as soon as I said it.

Luna's figure stirred. She stood up, gracefully as ever, and ran over to me, jumping over candles. She grabbed a towel from the floor, putting it over the spot where my pants were burning. After the fire had gone out, she sighed.

The sudden brightness made my eyes hurt and I saw that Luna wasn't comfortable by the brightness of the lights above our head, either. Luna got a cup from the kitchen, putting it over each and every candle until the fire gave up, the smoke being the only evidence of the fire's fight to stay alive. Luna carried the cup back to the kitchen. Once she came back, she closed her eyes, sighing for a moment, then coming over to me. She looked guilty. Or was it something else?

"Oscar--"

"Tell me." I whispered.

"I did something I'm not supposed to do," sobbed Luna.

"What?"

"I overheard two Magistratus officers talking. The ship's radars have detected a planet. A hospitable planet. And we're going to land there."

Relief coursed through my veins, my heart pumping faster and faster. We were going to get out of this place. Even I knew that the ship's radar's were designed to detect hospitable planets. Hospitable planets where there was oxygen to breathe, greens to use, and people to socialize with. But how could people be on the planet. Every human was on the Super Astra. Almost every human.

"But why do you look guilty. You should be happy! We're going to get out of this place!"

Luna shook her head.

"I can hear them, though. Their thoughts."

"What? Whose thoughts?"

"The people on the planet. I can hear their thoughts. All their thoughts. Even the ones I don't want to hear. Not that I want to hear any of them, but. . ."

"You can hear their thoughts?"

Luna nodded.

"Luna, what a nice game. Would you mind telling me the truth, now?"

"It is the truth, Oscar."

"I have some money saved up. Want to go to a psychologist?"

Luna's eyes widened. She crumbled on the ground, sobbing. What was she doing? Was she losing her mind or something?

"Oscar, this is the truth. I can hear them."

"And what are they thinking, Luna?"

"They're bloodthirsty. They'll kill us once they earn our trust. We. Will. All. Die."

Luna Russell

I squeezed my eyes shut, drops of sweat appearing on my temple. Oscar had left after I had told him about what I heard. He'd looked so scared. Scared of me.

I screamed, frustration bubbling inside me. Why? Why could I hear these people's thoughts? Why now?

Oh, goody. Little visitors coming. I haven't had the satisfaction of mental manipulation in years. Centuries!, screamed the mind of a middle-aged alien.

Everyone was thinking about mental manipulation. And killing.

I was losing my mind, for sure. There was no other explanation.

His lips are so plump. I wonder how it would feel to kiss him. Oh, he's looking at me that way. Oh. Oh!

And the thoughts that weren't plagued by the idea of killing everyone aboard the Super Astra, were filled with evil pleasure and more. Way more.

But maybe, I wasn't the only one losing my mind. What if I consulted my other friends?

I screamed again. I stood up, grabbing onto a chair to keep from wobbling. I walked to the door, slamming it behind me.

Noise didn't work. I could hear the people's thoughts no matter what. Even if a deafening bomb was exploding near me. I could still hear them. Even when I was banging on the metal pots and pans with stainless steel spoons. Nothing worked. I walked down the hallway, the urge to scream with frustration growing inside me.

A few minutes later, I found myself in front of Bella's door. I knocked once and was relieved when Bella opened, quickly. Her blonde hair fluttered by her face, her stunning blue eyes etched with frustration.

Bella looked skinnier than before, her skinny legs barely holding up her frail body. I wondered if I looked like that.

"Hey Luna," she said with a tired lethargic voice.

"Bella, we need to talk." I said.

Bella looked as if she was about to collapse.

"What's up?"

"I'm hearing things. Voices."

Bella's eyes widened.

"Come in." she ordered. I obeyed.

"Tell me."

I explained what was happening. The fact that we would soon land on a planet, which was harbored by humans, or human-like creatures. Creatures that looked human enough to fool the radar. I told Bella about the thoughts I was hearing. She put her head in her hands, exhaling with relief.

"So I'm not the only one going crazy, then?"

The comment shook me.

"What? Are you hearing--"

"No," said Bella with a stern expression. "I'm seeing things. Gruesome scenes of our future."

My eyes widened. If that was happening, then. . .

"I see a man with bloodshot eyes in the center of a circle. He's saying words or phrases, I can't tell. Once he says something, the people around him scream and fall. Some keep squirming on the ground, others get handed knives. They all die. Then. . ."

"No! Stop! Please! I don't need to know more!"

Bella looked at me, sympathy in her expression.

Suddenly, the doors burst open, to kids my age running in. Their pitch black hair was wild, their purple eyes debossed with fear. The boy was pale, his purple eyes wide. The girl next to him was trembling ever so slightly. Their toothpick-like bodies looking like dominos, ready to topple over.

"Esme? Oliver? What--"

"We're going crazy!" screamed Esme.

"Welcome to the club," I muttered. The boy looked at me with disgust. The girl with fear.

"What's happening?" asked Bella, calmly. She stood up, her frail body trembling with effort.

"We don't know, yet." stuttered Esme. "I. . . I feel a tingling in my palms. I just won't stop. And Oliver gets vibrations in his chest. At one point, we were alone in a room, and we thought there was an earthquake, the vibrations were so strong!"

Bella's eyes widened.

Oscar Smith

I walked down the hallway, my eyes darting left and right. The ship's radars had detected a hospitable planet with human-like creatures. And Luna could hear their voices. Their thoughts. What they were thinking. It was nonsense. This couldn't be true. How could you hear someone's thoughts? Especially when the Super Astra crew just announced that the planet was two hundred seventy six miles from us.

I sighed. Everything was going crazy. Even Luna, the girl I loved and adored was starting to go crazy. And I could do nothing to help her. I didn't know how to help her. I needed to talk to someone.

A long list of names formed in my head. Tanya North. Nah. I didn't need to talk to my childhood crush. Luna Russell. The crazy one. My dad. I would probably find him asleep in some pub.

After scrolling down the list of names, Bella's name appeared. Bella. That was it. Bella was understanding. She would help me. I knew she could help me.

I started running through the sterile hallways, straightening my mask as the doors and lights blurred beside me. It was not long before I found myself standing in front of Bella's apartment, catching my breath.

While steadying my breath, I heard frantic voices, shushed with the fear of getting uncovered by the Magistratus. Was Bella doing something illegal?

Not likely.

I knocked on the door, waiting for the distant footsteps to get closer and closer. Finally, the door opened, revealing Bella, her beautiful golden hair bouncing around the sides of her face. The hair was the only thing that looked alive, though. Her ocean blue eyes, were rimmed with fear. Her skinny, frail figure trembled as she tried to hold herself up. Bella smiled, then sighed.

"Come in." she said.

I walked into the apartment, similar to my own, only a bit simpler. There was less furniture in the living room, the people in the room, sitting on the floor. I spotted a girl, looking exactly like the boy next to her. Pitch black hair and wondrous purple eyes. I wondered if they wore colored contacts. The boy shifted, his frail body trembling with effort. The girl looked as if she was about to collapse.

Next to them was Luna. I was tempted to turn around and run out of the door. Bella shut the door, smiling apologetically.

Luna's scooted aside, leaving a blank space on the floor. It was where I was supposed to sit. It was where I wasn't going to sit. My eyes searched the room, falling on an empty chair. There were no other chairs in the room, the fact making me want to occupy it even more.

I walked toward the chair, sensing everyone's eyes on me. Someone coughed, and with a jolt, I realized that this was Bella's seat. I turned around, seeing Bella behind me. She smiled, and whispered, "You can have it. I'll sit on the floor."

Bella sat on the floor, next to the boy. A twinge of pain rang in my ears. I was so selfish. Bella was so frail. She needed to sit on a chair, and I took it away from her. I looked at Bella, our eyes locking for a moment. Bella nodded encouragingly and I sat down, my eyes avoiding Luna's piercing blue ones.

Luna cleared her throat.

"So. . ."

"Are you losing your sanity as well?" asked the boy. I looked at him in horror. Surely Luna was the only one going crazy. Was it contagious? Or was everyone in the room crazy?

"What? Aughhhhhhhh!" I screamed, clutching my temple with both hands. A stabbing pain pierced through my brain, like a butcher knife through skin. Like a hot knife through a butter. The pain continued, and when it subsided, it left a small nagging pain.

I didn't realize I had toppled out of the chair, until I noticed everyone leaning over me, like I was something to inspect.

"Oh gosh! We should probably get Krystal!" screamed the girl. "Oliver, move!"

"Esme, no!" yelled Oliver as he grasped Esme's wrist, his bones sticking out against his pale skin.

Vibrations coursed through my brain, leaving me with a never-ending headache. I heard a low moan. Who was it?

Esme fluttered over to my side, and I realized the moan had escaped *my* lips.

"What's happening?" asked Bella. "Oscar, tell us. What do you feel?"

"Awful pain. Vibrations. Then a nagging pain. Headache. It's all in my--"

A piercing scream stabbed at my brain. I could tell it was a girl. A very young girl. She was going to die. She was on this ship. I had no idea how I knew all this, but I willed the torture to stop. I willed her scream to die. If there was any way I could cover her with a shield or something to preserve her life. I could tell something was controlling her, causing her intolerable pain to run inside her like an electric shock. But that wasn't all her pain. She was weak-minded, the barriers around her sanity weak and now, evaporating. Something was controlling her arms, making her plunge the knife deeper and deeper into her chest. Then the screams died.

I gasped and sat up, looking around frantically for the source of the scream. Bella's arms were around me, holding me up as my body trembled. Next to her, Oliver had his arms around Esme, whose eyes were shut with concentration and whose face was red with effort. Luna looked as if she'd been split in two. She was standing between me and Esme, like a bridge between two islands. She looked around frantically, wondering where she should go. Who she should help first. Our eyes locked and she rushed over to my side, whispering encouraging comments. Luna looked at Bella, and a silent message passed between them. Bella rushed over to Esme's side, rubbing her shoulders.

Esme's eyes flew open and she screamed. Her scream blended into the little girl's second scream. I could barely tell the difference between the girl's screams and Esme's screams. The screaming slowly ate away at my confidence, making me think that whatever was attacking the ship, would take me down, as well. *Nonsense!* Scolded a part of my brain, *You are stronger than you think!*

I willed myself to keep calm and gain confidence. The hollow empty feeling in my chest was quickly replaced with a calm and confident one. I was proud of my mental abilities as I kept the shield up long enough for the screams to stop. I opened my eyes, but my happiness soon vanished as I found Luna, Bella, Esme, and Oliver on the floor, writhing in pain. I rushed to Bella, my arms engulfing her. She opened her eyes and stared at me with a hollow, longing look.

"I saw it." she whispered, her body trembling with effort as she stood up. "Oscar, I saw the outcome. I saw the girl dying before she died. And. . . I saw the person who killed her."

I stared at her.

Luna was soon next to us, rubbing her head. She had a panicked look on her face, her eyes wide with terror. Luna looked at Bella, sharing a silent message, before running to Esme and Oliver. Oliver was shivering near Esme, while his sister lay spread eagle on the floor as her blank eyes stared up at the ceiling.

Bella and Luna rushed to Esme's side, leaving me with no choice but to go to Oliver.

Oliver was trembling, his lips blue and his face red. I was about to go get a blanket from somewhere, warm him up, and comfort him before a rattling BOOM echoed across the ship. The ship rattled again, making me slam my head onto the floor. My cry was muffled by a second explosion and then by the sound of the exit ramp lowering.

The noises stopped, only to be followed by the artificial female voice, issuing commands.

"Citizens of Imperium, I now welcome you to the planet we shall be harboring. For your safety, please take all your belongings. You have 24 hours to take all of your belongings and--"

The artificial female voice abruptly cut off.

"Welcome to Spero! This is King Anton, King of Spero--" said a gruff voice before it was cut off by a higher, squeakier voice, belonging to a woman. "And this is Queen Leto, Queen of Spero! Please, do not bother for your luggage. Our faithful servants here will take everything to the loading docks. For now, please join us in the Great Hall of our breathtaking castle. *Vide te mox!*"

I looked at my friends. Esme had stood up, and was now trembling against Oliver, who looked as if he was about to fall down. Bella and Luna were holding hands in order to even out the weight between them.

"What happened?" I asked, looking around for answers. "When the girl was--"

Esme closed her eyes, as all her weight fell on Oliver. He started trembling more violently now but held her up.

"I tried to push the harm away from her." whispered Esme, opening her eyes only to display a showcase of terror and shame. "It worked, for a moment, but then my energy snapped. She. . . she died!"

Luna walked over to Esme.

"Luna," she said, sticking her hand out.

"Esme," whispered Esme.

"I feel for you. I had the evil person's thoughts in my head the whole time. The person who was torturing the little girl. I've never heard anything so dark and vile. He took pleasure in her pain," sobbed Luna, collapsing on the floor.

Bella rushed over to Luna's side, hugging her and comforting her.

"I saw the outcome of the whole thing. Her death. . . it was horrible!" sobbed Bella as she started sobbing into Luna's shoulder.

Oliver started talking about how he felt freezing cold the whole time. How he sensed a bad presence on the ship, but I didn't pay any attention to it. The girl had died. And I couldn't do anything about it because all I was doing was blocking the force from crumbling my sanity. I was thinking of myself, when people like Esme were trying to stop the tragedy.

Now I knew what it was to be insane. We were all doing supernatural things we couldn't before. We had powers. We had gifts. Gifts that would probably cost us our sanity. Gifts we could do nothing about.

Sam Grey

I punched the wall in frustration, not caring that my fingers were cracking. They would heal, just like everything else. All my bruises, all my cuts, all my sprains, and even the fractures in my fingers, healed instantly. Ever since we landed on the new planet. Everything healed instantly.

I heard a knock just as I was about to exit the room. Who could it be? My parents had escaped the ship, as soon as possible, leaving me to take anything of great value. You never knew what these *people* would steal.

I hurried over to the door, jumping over the pile of things that fell down during the landing procedure. I opened it, preparing myself to fight whatever or whoever had come. Once I opened the door, though, I couldn't fight. I could only stare. Stare at the humanoid creature standing before me. It was a young woman, her auburn hair glinting in the light of the lights. The girl bowed her head once, then looked up, her startling green eyes sending an electric shock down my spine. I cringed. The girl wore a silver dress that covered her arm, most of her neck, and all of her legs, but outlined her round stomach perfectly. She was pregnant. Really pregnant. I tore my eyes from her bulging stomach and focused on her. The girl smiled.

"Sam Grey, I am delighted to see you." she said in a robotic voice, making me wonder if she was an escort droid. But they didn't make escort droids this pretty. This beautiful. And escort droids couldn't be pregnant. Or could they? No one knew what the government was doing these days.

The girl moved forward, her movements fast and blurry. She grabbed me by the wrist, the electric shock returning to my spine.

A vision of something, something that didn't belong to me, filled my head. Once I focused, I saw the girl's childhood.

Suddenly, I was a young girl of the age of thirteen. I ran to the window and once I saw the Ufficiali, the officers, marching toward our hut. I ran back, clinging to my mother's skirts. The Ufficiali burst in, issuing commands. They swarmed around the hut, filling up every available space. The Capo, or the boss, came forward, holding a Tavoletta. That little tablet expressed such light, there was no need of the candles floating around. I saw the Capo's knuckles, white, as they clutched the Tavoletta with such force. As if he worried that I would see all the confidential government information stored within it.

"Elina Saar, we are glad to inform you that Her Majesty, Queen Leto and His Majesty, King Anton have picked you to be a royal servant." announced The Capo, smiling at my fear. Beside him stood a dozen Ufficiali, showing no hint of emotion. The Capo turned to my mother, whose face was white with terror. "Estera Saar, please say goodbye to your daughter."

My mother nodded, as she turned to me, grabbing my shoulders and looking me in the eyes.

"Elina, don't let them do anything to you. Don't let them do anything without your consent." she ordered, her eyes tearing up. "I love you, Elina, and I always will. Now do what they tell you, stay away from the Ufficiali, especially The Capo, stay away from the King, and . . . you know what?" My mother paused, before raising her voice so the Capo could hear her. "For Spero!"

The Ufficiali took me away, leading me through a maze of underground corridors, our shadows lingering and flickering behind us as the electric torch flickered on and off. The two Ufficiali officers marched beside me, their gazes far, far away. I wondered what their were thinking about. Maybe they were thinking about their families. Or maybe they would think of the ways to torture me into accepting the Royal family's restrictions.

I sighed, the sound of surrender echoing through the barren corridors. One of the Ufficiali smirked. Yep, he was definitely thinking about torturing me.

We walked for a long time, our footsteps making a constant tapping noise against the cold, stone floor. The corridor opened into a large chamber. Golden chandeliers hung from the ceiling and platinum rimmed candles hung over my head. The stone floor turned to marble and I no longer had to watch out for tree roots that had grown through the cracks. A podium rose out of nowhere, two elaborate golden thrones perched on top. A platinum blonde woman with rosy cheeks and emerald green eyes, smiled at me. She wore a dazzling purple gown with a diamond necklace. She was perched on top a throne and wore a beautiful silver crown. I realized that this was Queen Leto. An electric current ran down my spine as I looked over to King Anton.

He had platinum blond hair, and like his wife, also had emerald green eyes. He looked at me with amusement, as his eyes ran all over my body. I cringed and had the sudden urge to hide. King Anton wore robes made out of Ferrox, the only natural resource found on Spero. Everything else- the gold on the chandeliers, the platinum on the candles, the silver on Queen Leto's crown, and the bronze on King Anton's throne was all shipped from Fidem- Spero's sister planet. All the food and all the water was all from Fidem. Everything except Ferrox was from Fidem. Everything.

Queen Leto cleared her throat and her vibrant smile turned into a smirk. Her eyes scanned my body, but not like King Anton. She wasn't appreciating my details and curves. She was smirking at my excuse for a dress.

The Ufficiali made me sit on a copper chair facing the thrones. King Anton's eyes never me, making me feel uncomfortable and vulnerable.

"The Protocol of Serving Spero states that 'One must serve Spero no matter what. Even the lowly servants must serve Spero in time of war and need'. Do you, Elina Severa Saar, pledge to do anything to serve Spero?"

I felt my body and mind bend against Queen Leto's will and I heard myself saying, "I do."

"Do you pledge to do anything that may please the King or the Queen?"

I looked at King Anton as he seemed to be enjoying this bit of the pledging. I focused once more on Queen Leto's words. No, I wouldn't do anything to please the royal family. They could want me to do anything to please them. Anything. But before I could say my own words, my lips parted, revealing the words, "I do."

"Do you swear to obey all the laws of Spero?"

"I do,"

The pledging went by quickly and soon I found myself in a large chamber with multiple torture devices. The Ufficiali escorted me to a deadly-looking machine. The machine resembled a closet, only there were metal straps to keep your neck, hands, waist, and feet from moving. The door was swung outward, revealing a set of sharp needles embedded into the inside of the door. I gulped, waiting for Queen Leto to announce the worse. Death. Had I not pleased her enough by pledging to the royal family of Spero?

"Manipulation," announced Queen Leto as the Ufficiali pushed me inside.

The rest was a daze. I remembered no part of it until the Ufficiali unbuckled the straps and sent me toward another machine. I looked around, amazed that I was now able to see more colors, hear more things, and smell more. I felt stronger than ever. The machine the Ufficiali lead me to smelled like a strong chemical, the smell burning my nostrils.

"And now," announced Queen Leto. "Eliminating every source of mind manipulation."

Mind manipulation?

Servants were purposefully picked weak in the mind so that they could be controlled. Very few even had a gift. Most were just ungifted, making them a disgrace to Spero. Making them useless. That's why they were serving the royal family as servants. But I had a small gift. And I didn't want to lose it.

I thrashed around while the Ufficiali were injecting needles into my veins. I thrashed and reached out with my mind but was surprised to find that no viterelectric waves were projecting from the Ufficiali's bodies. Their mental manipulation had been extracted, so they had no mental control over me. The thought reassured me, but just as I was gaining confidence, I felt my will bend. King Anton soothed my mind, his mind seeping into all of the cracks in mine. His manipulation slipped by all the mental barriers I had been trying to create ever since I was seven. He soothed and calmed me, making me feel more relaxed than ever. More relaxed than I should've been. He let me feel secure and happy. I tried fighting him but it was no use.

When I came out of the machine, everything seemed duller. The colors I used to see before were now limited to a rusty red, a yellow, a dusty blue, and a dull green. I couldn't hear as many things as before and I smelled nothing but the toxic chemicals in the chamber.

The Ufficiali lead me through the servant chambers, leaving me with a bundle of clothes and nothing to do.

Elina's life started speeding up, and I only got flashes of her life.

When she was personally thanked by Queen Leto for her faithful service over the years..

When she got her first Ufficiali boyfriend.

When her mother died.

When her younger sister, Amara joined the royal servants.

Elina's life kept on speeding up until it stopped, at moment full of terror and despair.

I walked the hallway, a bundle of towels in my arms. I watched as the figure of King Anton came from behind the corner, a confident smile on his face. As he drew near, I bowed, balancing the towels in one hand, as I placed the other hand behind my back as I bowed.

King Anton gently took the towels from my hand. I looked up in surprise and alarm. With his pointer finger he lifted my chin, so that I was looking right at him. At his cruel face. I flinched violently as he ordered me to come with him. He sped down the hallway leaving me puzzled and terrified.

The scenes whizzed past my mind before stopping again.

I rubbed my bulging stomach as I sat in the servant's chambers. This child, this thing inside me was foreign to me. Seeter, my Ufficiali boyfriend had left me behind for this wasn't his creation. It was the King's.

The next scenes were terrifying and I quickly tore Elina's hand from my wrist. The connection broke instantly. She gaped at me in terror. Then in amazement. Then in confusion.

"Gifted," mumbled Elina, as she ran away from me.

Esme Hall

We walked through the palace hallways, our footsteps making synchronized taps on the cold marble floor. New strength coursed through my veins, making me feel strong but unsure of myself. We were in a foreign planet. Anything could be a trap, something to lure us to death. After all, we'd landed mere moments after that little girl was killed. These people, these humanoid creatures could've killed her for all we know.

Luna sighed. Her sigh was quick and full of fear. All our powers had strengthened once we stepped on the planet. Our strength had returned, our frail bodies returning to normal. The crowded corridor soon opened into a vast room, full of decorations and small details that made that palace look grand and exotic. The platinum walls now held paintings of people posing in strange poses instead of floating candles. Some of the people were upside down, as if the portrait had been turned upside down. Other people were just in strange poses, like that one lady who was doing a headstand with a golden gown on.

The floor now contained golden-rimmed tiles made of jade. The room smelled of fresh-baked pastries. The smell made my mouth water, but I pushed everything away as I tried to focus on the other details of the room. In the corners were small, potted palm trees, their branches waving as the air conditioner blared above them. Long, elaborate tables were placed along the walls, their silk tablecloths glistening in the light of the golden chandeliers hanging overhead. Dishes of exotic and exquisite food had been gently placed onto plates made of an expensive mineral. Feltspar, I think.

A large podium rose and on it were perched two thrones containing two people. The woman had platinum blonde hair which was pulled into a braid that hung over her shoulder. Her bright emerald eyes scanned the crowd as she looked for confusion she might be able to solve. Once her eyes landed on us, though, they stopped moving, zeroing in on us. She scowled and patted the guy who was sitting next to her on the shoulder. He looked at her, his expression slightly annoyed. The lady whispered something in his ear, and his eyes automatically found us. He scowled, but waved her warnings away as if we weren't important enough.

The woman straightened her silver crown and schooled her expression. Next to her, the guy stood up from his broze throne, making a small gesture at the woman. She scowled once again, but stood up, fixing her ruby red dress so that she looked thinner. Which wasn't possible because she was extremely pregnant.

"Dear Earthen Guests," announced the guy in a gruff voice. He seemed familiar, or at least his voice did. "Welcome to Spero! I am King Anton Hale, king of Spero and--"

"--and I am Queen Leto Hale, queen of Spero! Please feel free to eat anything you want, for it is there for you. The people of Spero welcome you with open arms but we are sorry to inform you that--"

Queen Leto was cut off, King Anton's gruff voice taking her place.

"--we are sorry to inform you that because the palace is not big enough, anyone who is not part of a Star family must stay with one of the Aristocratic families. Spero has over a hundred Aristocratic families so feel free to knock on any door. Our families would gladly provide shelter for you." said King Anton, as he smiled.

"Is it a girl or a boy?" yelled a young girl from beside the dessert tables. Her face was covered in chocolate as she munched on a chocolate croissant. The question took everyone by surprise and the smile vanished from King Anton's face. His face went pale as he looked over at a pregnant servant standing near him. The servant held up a plate of fruit and I wondered what dirty secret the servant and the King shared. Queen Leto, however, smiled vibrantly as she rubbed her bulging stomach.

"Its a girl, sweetie." said the King. The girl suddenly forgot her croissant and looked at the queen's bulging stomach in awe.

"What's her name?" asked the young girl, the croissant dropping from her hand and onto the floor. The pregnant servant rushed over, picking up the croissant and brushing the carpet to make sure no crumbs were left.

"Cedrica Apolonia Hale." answered the Queen. Queen Leto smiled, sending an electric shock down my spine. As soon as it was over I had a sudden urge to admire the Queen for all that she had overcome. She was soon going to give birth to a beautiful baby girl that would one day become Spero's queen. Queen Leto smiled and I noticed how pretty she was. Beautiful platinum blonde hair and stunning emerald green eyes. I wanted to look over, to see if my friends were in a similar trance but I couldn't. The Queen was too beautiful. No wonder the King had chose her as his Queen. Oscar tapped me on the shoulder and it took an infinite amount of energy to tear my eyes away from the Queen's perfect heart-shaped face. I looked over at Oscar. His lips were moving but no sound was coming out. As a glass wall was separating us. I wondered what he could be possibly saying but it was like somebody had tapped the mute button. As Oscar kept on yelling and waving his arms around, I started to panic. What was happening?

I felt all the blood drain from my face, as I realized that the Queen was probably controlling us. No, she was controlling us. Manipulating us. I squeezed my eyes shut, straining my ears to hear anything that may indicate that someone was controlling us. Maybe a grunt. Something to indicate that manipulating 17 billion people was giving them a hard time. No matter how hard I listened, I couldn't hear a thing. But I could swear that someone was controlling us, meaning that they could make us do anything. *Anything.*

I concentrated harder, and tried to wrap a shield or something to avoid the manipulation. I could feel my mind stretching into Luna's. Then into Oscar's. Then into Oliver's. And finally into Bella's. Their mental barriers let me through and when I opened my eyes, we were all surrounded by a translucent bright green bubble. It was enough to see through. I could see the dazed faces surrounding us as they gaped at Queen Leto's surprised face. Next to her, King Anton was scowling as he pounded a fist into his hand. I looked around and was relieved to see that

Oliver, Bella, and Luna were back to normal again. They stared at the bubble surrounding us, then turning to me for explanations I couldn't give.

I shut my eyes once again and focused on keeping the shield up. It was easier than when I tried to protect the little girl. My brain easily concentrated and soon keeping the shield up was something I didn't have to think about much. I opened my eyes, and realized that the people around us no longer had dazed faces. They mingled around us, either ignoring the bright green bubble surrounding us or not seeing it at all. The King and Queen gaped at us. I felt uncomfortable and vulnerable even though, their manipulation wasn't enough to penetrate the shield.

The pregnant servant rushed over to us. Her face looked strained as her skinny body looked like it was about to collapse. *The weight of her enormous stomach must be tiring her,* I thought.

"Follow me." she whispered as she turned around toward the Great Hall's exit. I reluctantly looked at my friends, knowing that we would have to move together in order for all of us to stay in the shield. Luna nodded, and I realized that we should trust her the most. She could hear what was in people's minds. She would know their true intentions. I looked over at Bella, relieved when she nodded as well, as if she'd seen the outcome of all this.

We walked toward the exit and were soon lead past so many hallways, that I was sure we were on the other side of the palace. Finally, the girl turned around, nodding once. I got the impression that she wanted the shield to drop, and so it did.

I felt uncovered and vulnerable without it, but if Bella and Luna trusted her, than so should I.

"You're gifted." said the girl, as she looked at us with wary eyes. She was beautiful and it was obvious she wasn't human, but something about her just wasn't right. "Meaning you don't have mind manipulation. Instead you have another supernatural power. A power that very few have. Meaning, you've descended from gifted people. You're great, great, great, great, great parents are the Ancient Gifted People of Spero."

"The what of Spero?" asked Oliver, as his eyes widened.

"The Ancient Gifted People of Spero." repeated the servant.

"Cool." muttered Oscar as he and Oliver exchanged uninterested glances.

"Not exactly. You don't have mental manipulation. Instead you have other gifts."

"We know that, but why?" asked Bella as she pulled her hair back.

"Your ancestors are the Ancient Gifted People of Spero." said the servant, before she paused to look at Bella and Luna.

"I see." said Luna, as if she was reading the servant's thoughts. She probably was, but still. Luna turned to us. "King Anton and Queen Leto. . . right, sorry. I didn't know names had power. The King and Queen claimed that the people of Spero were safe because the gifted people died out a long time ago, leaving no descendents to cause interference. But in reality, the Gifted people were getting hunted, so they escaped to Earth." Luna paused, a turned around to look at the servant. She nodded encouragingly, as her eyes swept over Oliver. "The farther they went, the more their Gifts weakened. Once they landed on Earth, their Gifts vanished which made them blend into society. The Gifts were passed down from generation to generation, though no one knew.--"

"How do you know, then?" I asked, curiosity coursing through my veins.

"Everyone knows," whispered the servant.

"But-"

The girl smiled weakly as she ran her hand over her bulging stomach.

"But do you have mental manipulation abilities or whatever?" I asked reluctantly.

"I don't have manipulation. I can only be manipulated."

The servant's bright green eyes clouded over with sadness.

"Can I finish?" asked Luna, frustrated. We all nodded and Luna finished her story. "Now that we're on Spero, the Gift has come back. The gift was coming back when were on the Super Astra but we couldn't be *on* Spero, so we were getting weak."

"Precisely." said the servant. "You read minds very well for a beginner."

Luna blushed, but stayed silent.

"Anything else we should know?" asked Oscar.

"Well, every person from Spero has the ability to heal momentarily. It is something that cannot be extracted from the brain. Your little friend has discovered that ability." said the servant. She lead us toward a door, which was cracked slightly open. The servant pushed the door open, revealing a boy leaning against a wall. He was my age, had startling platinum blond hair, and chocolate brown eyes. His eyes warily ran over each of us, before they stopped at me. He smiled, and stuck his hand out as if we were in a business meeting. "I don't advise touching him."

I looked around.

The room was small, containing a bed, a bedside table, a wardrobe, and a lamp. Otherwise, the room was bare, which send an eerie feeling down my spine.

"Sam?" asked Bella, reluctantly. She walked a few steps forward, then stopped.

"Hey Bella." Sam said in a casual way that made me wonder why he was so calm about all *this*. "Who are your friends here?"

Bella took a step forward, then paused, chewing nervously on her lip. She looked at me and I nodded, hoping to encourage her to be braver.

"This is Esme and her twin brother Oliver," said Bella as she pointed at me, then at Oliver. "This is Luna. And Oscar." pointed out Bella.

Sam nodded and stuck his hand out, disappointment obvious on his face every time we kindly refused. The servant must've had a reason to warn us. Sam frowned and looked over to the servant.

"Elina, what have you told them?" asked Sam. "It doesn't work on humans. It works only on Fures."

"Wait, what?" asked Oliver, his eyes widening.

Elina cleared her throat, looking uncomfortable.

"Sam's Gift is peculiar. He can touch you and he knows your whole life story." said Elina, as she looked down at her bulging stomach. "Apparently it doesn't work on humans, only on Fures."

"And Fures are?"

"Fures is the name for people from Spero." said Elina, pausing once she saw the confusion on our faces. "Humans don't call themselves Earthens, they call themselves humans. We don't call ourselves Speroans, we're Fures."

"I see." said Luna, eyeing Sam with a questioning look. "Our gifts work only on Fures, as well. I mean, I can't read my friends' thoughts, but. . . I can read Elina's thoughts."

I watched as Elina flinched as if someone was stabbing her with a knife.

"You'll need to hide. The King and Queen won't stop searching for you. They'll hunt you down to preserve their reputation." explained Elina, rubbing her hand over her stomach once again. "I think I know where you can hide."

"Are we going to hide with Amara?" asked Sam, as he looked at me with greedy eyes. Our eyes locked and he smiled, blushed, and looked in Elina's direction. "Your sister? Are we going to hide with her?"

Elina flinched as her eyes teared up.

"Don't. Just don't push it further." said Luna, her voice filled with sympathy. "The subject pains her."

"No. You deserve to know. My younger sister conceived the King's child. They executed her before she could give birth. They executed her because her child would be born before the Queen's meaning that her child would rule Spero first." said Elina as she brushed a tear aside. "She was going to give birth to a beautiful baby boy." Elina looked at Sam, and smiled weakly. "I thought you knew every bit of my life. Apparently you don't get the whole story with one touch."

"And. . . and you? What'll happen to you?" asked Sam. "You concieved the King's child, as well."

Elina smiled.

"My dear boy. Evangelina will be born after the Queen's child. She'll be born after Cedrica." said Elina, as she rubbed her stomach once again. "I'll be fine. As long as Evangelina doesn't try to claim the Hale surname or the throne."

"Evangelina? Is that what your baby is going to be called?" asked Bella.

"Yes." said Elina, her face suddenly turning serious as stone. "Now let's discuss where you'll hide."

Elina Saar

"The King and Queen saw that I took you away from the Great Hall. They saw that I helped you, so you'll no longer be safe if you stay with me." I explained. "I'll soon be executed for helping you. I have two half-sisters that would be willing to give you temporary shelter."

I looked at the kids, taking in all their beautiful faces, thinking of how these little creatures could possibly be related to me. How these little bodies could hold a Gift so strong and powerful, that even the King and Queen were scared of their abilities.

"You have a choice." I continued explaining. "You can either stay with with Paris or with Aurora."

The kids stared at me, their expressions longing for explanations.

"Paris is a third tier Adiutor. Meaning she helps the royal family with the most minor tasks possible. Aurora doesn't work. She's married to a first tier Adiutor meaning that he carries out the most important tasks. Andre's rarely home. You'll be safer at Aurora's house because she won't be suspected. She's a woman with no manipulation living in the outskirts of the main city."

The kids stirred and one of them, the one with beautiful blonde hair and stunning blue eyes, cleared her throat.

"Before we pick-"

"Wouldn't it be better if we knew Paris and Aurora's stories. I mean, no offense, but if one of them has a criminal record, the King and Queen are most likely to search there." said the girl with strange hair and ice blue eyes. How can someone have hair that weird? Not exactly brown. But not dirty blonde.

I took a deep breath as I rubbed my bulging stomach. I could feel a lump, a foot or an arm, moving throughout the stomach, the movement sending eerie chills down my senseless spine. Over the years, my senses dulled. Having no manipulation to freshen and strengthen my senses had a toll on my whole body. I could now see more colors than right after the manipulation extraction procedure, but every sense was still dull.

"My father was away most of the time, for he was an Ufficiali officer." I began, the words escaping my mouth before I could think through them. "My mother was a happy woman, most of the time, atleast. Together they had Amara, Alyssa, and me."

I took a deep breath.

"I was the oldest child, Amara was second. When I was seven or so, my parents had Alyssa. She was born skinny and frail, basically on the brink of death. A couple hours after she was born, Alyssa died. Our father left us for he said that our mother couldn't produce strong children anymore. A couple months later, we found out that a woman named, Lia, was pregnant with our father's child. Paris was born a few months later. She was a nice girl, and I liked her. It wasn't her fault that the father we shared was an idiot. Paris was born with a pretty strong manipulative ability, so our father was proud. He entered her in a tournament to see who had the most promising manipulative ability. Paris ended up third. The King saw something in her, maybe it was beauty or skill but he gave her a place with the royal Adiutors."

The group stirred making me feel uncomfortable for some reason.

"A couple months after Paris was born, we discovered that our father had an affair with a woman named Aura. Aurora was born with no manipulation abilities. She married a first tier Adiutor and now had a couple kids. Three, I think."

"I see," said the girl with the black hair. She looked slightly confused for a moment before focusing on me. "This is off topic and all, but while we were on the ship, there was a deadly pandemic that broke out. Do you by any chance know what will happen to us? I mean, we just left the ship."

I frowned.

"The King and Queen ordered for that disease to be manufactured in special research facilities." I said, keeping my voice steady. "They somehow managed to send another supply of food to Earth. The food, though, was plagued with Mortemisis microbes. That's how the disease started. We, Fures, are immune to these microbes. I don't know what they'll do with your contaminated ship, though."

The girl with weird hair and icy eyes swayed a little bit, which made the boy with black hair and purple eyes scoot aside. The girl gulped then looked at me. The mind-reader gasped.

The girl's face went white as she fainted, her limp body collapsing on the hard floor. Everyone fluttered around her, desperate to help the mind reader. Everyone except Sam. He looked at me with wide eyes, with desperation.

"But why would they do that?" he asked, as he crouched down next to the mind reader. "Why would they manufacture a disease and send that to humans? To kill us?"

I sighed.

"I'm afraid the goal was to weaken you." I whispered. "So that you would be desperate and come to Spero. So that they could manipulate you and kill you."

Someone gasped.

"Oh!" shrieked the blonde girl, as she shook the mind reader's limp shoulders. "Oh no! No, no, no! Luna wake up!"

The mind reader was pale, unresponsive, and limp. Almost as if she were lifeless.

Luna Russell

My eyes fluttered open. Around me was darkness, though I could see soft halos belonging to lights on both of my sides. I could hear the steady drip of water, I could feel the hard rock beneath my fingers as I ran my fingers along the walls, and I could hear creatures scurrying in the darkness. I was in cave.

I frantically looked around, my eyes searching for an exit. To my left was an opening, through which I could see a grassy green hill. The sunshine gleamed in the horizon as the pink clouds drifted in the orange sky. It was sunset, meaning that soon the gateway to freedom would close. I did not know how I knew this, but nagging voice in my mind informed me that if I were to survive the night, I would need to go through this gateway.

I started walking toward the exit, my feet creating steady taps against the rocky floor, before a soft, mellow voice called out. I turned around, expecting to see another human in the cave with me.

To my right was light so dim, I could barely see it. The light blinked in a weak manor, informing me that the life source was draining out. I reluctantly walked over to the where the light stood. It wasn't just any light but a light shaped like a human. As I neared, I noticed that this was a ghost-like presence resembling a teenage girl around the age of seventeen. Though the figure was dim and almost transparent, I could make out the girl's platinum blonde hair, green eyes, silver crown, and sad smile. She wore a pale gown that had no color to describe it. In the middle of the gown sat a dark stain that ruined the girl's long-lost beauty. The dark liquid oozed out of her, like a lazy waterfall, evaporating once it hit the cavernous floor.

Somehow, I knew this was a memory, not exactly a phantom or a ghost but all that remained of the girl. She had something left behind in this world, through which her soul and essence could attach to. Something that helped someone remember her.

The girl smiled softly as she looked down at the bloody gash by her stomach. She then drifted passed me, her light slowly fading as she neared the exit. Curiosity coursed through my veins and I followed her. The girl turned around to face me as she gently drifted backwards, her back facing the exit. She smiled and headed toward the exit. I thought she would disappear, go into the paradise place where she would be happy for all eternity, before her light went out.

I scrambled around the cave, hoping to find the girl's memory again. As if on cue, a dim light appeared to my left, her light encasing soft shadows across the cavernous floor. Once she reached me, the girl stepped toward the cavern walls. Her hand touched the rock and suddenly, there was a beautiful ornate golden box in her hand. The girl walked toward me the sad smile still on her hollow face. She handed me the box, which felt icy cold in my grip. I looked at the girl reluctantly relieved when she nodded, obvious approval. I gently lifted the lid, my breath stopping once I saw the contents. In the box lay a golden locket in the shape of a delicate heart. The surface was smooth, but cold. I looked at the girl, confused for what I should be looking for, when it hit me. It was a locket. There was something important inside. Something that was important for me to know.

I opened the locket, a couple things popping out at once. On the inside of the locket the words, *Non solum iacentem protegens*, were inscribed. On the other side, was a folded piece of paper and below it was a picture of two young girls, my age, holding hands as they walked down a road.

I looked at the girl, relieved when she took the box from my hands. She smiled and handed me the locket.

"Read," said the girl, her voice soft and mellow. *"And look."*

I nodded once before I looked at the picture, the note laying in my other hand. In the picture the girls both had platinum blonde hair and stunning emerald green eyes. The girl on the left was taller and was obviously older. Both girls had vibrant smiles on their faces as if one had just said a funny joke. They wore matching royal blue gowns with golden flowers.

I hesitantly looked at the girl once again. She smiled encouragingly and took the locket from my hands. I looked down once again, remembering the forgotten note in my hand.

I gently unfolded the piece of paper, my eyes scanning over it. In the note lay another note, the other piece of paper tightly folded. The girl took the folded note, nodding once to tell me to read the note. I looked down and it took a second before my brain could decipher the fact that I was staring at a letter written by someone with neat handwriting.

Lies are just another version of the truth. Upgraded and new.

Before I knew what was going on, the folded piece of paper was in my hand, the other one gone. I gently unfolded the note, careful as not to rip it, and read the other message.

She loved me, but she didn't
She despised me, but she didn't
She drifted away from me, but she didn't
We were close, but we weren't

I looked at the girl, but she was already fading, her dim light blending into the darkness surrounding me. The girl smiled one last sad, hollow smile, then faded, leaving me in total darkness.

Bella Atherton

Luna's eyes fluttered open, her breaths coming in short, desperate gasps. As she sat up, beads of sweat trickled down her temple. Her icy eyes were wide with fear or shock, and her chin trembled. In her hands was a small, golden box that I didn't remember seeing before. The ornate lid, glinted in the Lux light that poured through the open window. On Spero they had a star called Lux that was providing light to the planet, same like our Sun use to be for the Earth.

"Where are we?" asked Luna in a small, confused voice. Her body trembled a bit and she reminded me of a newborn bird, weak and vulnerable. "Wha-what happened?"

"You fainted. We're still in the servant's chambers because we didn't want to make decisions without you." I explained, as I shut the window, the light momentarily disappearing as I drew the curtains.

A small light appeared in the center of the room, flickering weakly. Oliver neared us, the candle in his hand. Oliver's face looked pale and creepy as the fire played with the shadows on his face. Oscar sat in the corner, his eyes closed with concentration. Oscar was the only one here that couldn't be manipulated. Maybe it was a glitch in his brain, or maybe that was his supernatural power. I thought that it is his supernatural power. Being able to withstand mental manipulation was pretty supernatural. Esme and Oliver, on the other hand, thought that Oscar's power was just waiting to be discovered.

"Would you look at that? Sleeping beauty woke up." mused Oliver, as he neared us. "Bella, inform Luna what happened once she fainted."

"I did, Oliver." I whispered. Oliver's gaze met mine, and a shivery feeling passed over me. His startling purple eyes bore into my plain blue ones and and electric current crawled down my spine.

"No I mean the news." said Oliver.

"Right." I said, remembering our little discovery. "Luna, today's Oscar's birthday. And . . . we kind of missed my birthday, while we were on the ship. So everyone's fifteen. Except you."

"Wait what? What about Esme and Oliver?"

"We missed their birthday as well."

"So I'm the only one who's fourteen?"

"Yep," I said, worried that Luna may take this the wrong way. It's not good to be the youngest. Everyone thinks you're not worthy enough.

"Oh. That's not relevant, though. It's not important." said Luna with a confused expression. "Why are you telling me this?"

I heaved a sigh, relief flooding through me.

"Where's Elina?" asked Luna, as she tried to stand up, her legs wobbling with effort. I heard a soft, merry jingle coming from inside the golden box as its contents shifted. Luna's weary eyes scanned the dark, musty room; her icy blue eyes landing on each person in the room. "Where's Elina?" asked Luna, frustration obvious in her voice.

"Elina went back to the Great Hall." I said. "We're still in the servant's chambers. We didn't want to--"

"Make any decisions without me, I know." said Luna. Luna's eyes scanned the room once more, and she scowled. "Where's Sam?"

"He . . . he's exploring the castle." I answered, my voice soft and distant. I was worried. There were so many dangerous things out there, Sam might get hurt, or worse-die.

"But aren't we supposed to stay here? Aren't the King and Queen hunting us or something?" asked Luna, the scowl on her face deepening.

"I don't know." I admitted. Sam was so dark, secretive, and mysterious. The only thing I knew about him is that he had the ability of knowing someone's life story with just a touch. "I think he can fend for himself, though."

"True." muttered Luna. She started walking around the room, her footsteps making steady taps against the cold, stone floor.

"What's in that box?" I asked. I hadn't seen that box before. It's golden top gleamed in the dark, and I wondered if what lay beneath it was

Luna's or someone else's. "How'd you get it? I mean you didn't have it with you before, right?"

Luna turned to face me. She walked over in silence, her grim face dark and sad.

"I had a dream." whispered Luna. Slowly she explained everything that had happened in her dream. From the fact that she was in a cave with an exit to the fact that the ghost girl give her the box. "And, um, I just woke up with the box."

"Is the locket in the box?" I asked, as I eyed the ornate box with suspicion. What if the locket carried some kind of curse? I mean, I know that only happens in books, but still, I wondered if the ghost girl could be some kind of evil spirit haunting us. I wouldn't be surprised if it was like that. After all the mind manipulation, supernatural powers, new planets, and new relatives, I wouldn't be surprised if the ghost girl turned out to be Elina's mom (or something like that).

Luna's trembling hands slowly lifted the lid. A cold, vicious gust of air blasted through the room and even Oscar, who was in the corner turned to see what was happening. Luna's hand lifted a smooth locket in the shape of a delicate heart. It hung from a golden chain that looked as if it would fall apart soon. Though the locket looked preserved and new, it was obvious that it was ancient.

"Can you open it?" asked Oliver, the smirk on his face replaced with a surprised expression.

Luna slowly opened the locket, careful as not to drop the folded pieces of papers inside. She handed me a paper, then handed Oliver the other.

"There's something inscribed on the inside." said Luna. "*Non solum iacentem protegens*. What could that possibly mean?"

"I don't know." muttered Oliver, his eyes on his paper. He unfolded his paper and scowled. "*Lies are just another version of the truth. Upgraded and new*. Well that's stupid."

"Don't be so thick, Oliver." scolded Esme, as she neared us. "If it's in the locket, then it must be important. Bella, what does your paper say?"

"It's a poem." I said. I showed them the poem, careful to keep the box close so that it's light would help us see. Esme and Oliver read the poem; before looking over at Luna, their faces scrunched up in concerned glances.

"What does it mean?" asked Esme.

"I don't know." admitted Luna, as studied the paper. "But look at this."

Luna showed us the other side of the locket, the one with the picture. In it were two smiling little girls that looked like royalty.

"They look like they come from a royal family." I pointed out. "Look at those gowns. I don't think normal people in Spero wear such elaborate gowns."

"Royalty." mumbled Esme. "Other than Queen Leto and King Anton, there is no other royal family."

"There is no other royal family that we know of." pointed out Oliver.

"True," I muttered under my breath.

Luna's eyes widened as she gasped. We all turned to look at her, questioning glances hung on our faces. Seconds later, Sam burst through the door, his eyes wide as marbles. His face was red and he was panting like a dog left outside in a hot summer day.

"They're coming!" yelled Luna and Sam in synchronized way. We didn't bother asking questions, for we knew exactly who was coming. We burst through the open door and turned to right.

"Where're we going?" asked Oscar. I was startled to see him here, beside us. During the past couple hours, he just sat in the corner looking glum.

Just then, Luna opened her mouth as if she wanted to scream. Her eyes were wide with terror and her mouth was open, though no sound came out of her. She dropped onto her knees, then hit the ground. Her body twitched as if she had just been electrocuted, but otherwise she did not move. Or breath. Or blink. Or scream.

Esme screamed next, but instead of dropping to the stone floor, she froze in mid-step as she was trying to reach Luna. Unlike Luna, Esme was blinking and breathing, but her limbs stayed frozen. Esme's mouth quivered with effort as she tried to fight the force that had tied her tongue. Oliver dropped next to Esme. Unlike everyone else, Oliver's screams could be heard, even though they were muted. It was like a glass door separates us. I could hear Oliver, but just barely. I looked around frantically, as I searched for the person or perhaps the alien that was doing this.

Oscar seemed to be unaffected. He knelt by Luna as he tried to fix her, but I knew it wasn't that easy. Just then, my head burst open with pain. The pain was unbearable as it traveled down my spine, into my legs and back up.

In my head, I saw an army of Ufficiali storming toward us. In the middle walked the pregnant Queen Leto and her unfaithful husband. Both the Queen and the King had amused smiles on their faces as they walked toward us.

The scene changed, and I saw Elina's dead body splattered on the exquisite marble floor in The Great Hall. A bloody dagger protruded from her stomach, from the stomach where her unborn Evangelina lay. It was like someone splatter painted the floor with Elina's blood. Her glassy eyes were open, and she had a faraway smile on her face. Perhaps she thought of a good moment in her short life before the Queen had forced her to end her life.

The scene changed once again, and I saw our dead bodies laying against the cold stone floor. Luna's lungs had closed up, Esme's blood was running from her mouth, eyes, and ears, and Oliver's tongue forced its way down his throat and it blocked his airway. I lay on the floor by Oliver. My head was cracked open and my blood was creating a large blood red halo around me. Oscar was nowhere to be seen.

A scream of delight broke the vision and I could once again see reality. Queen Leto, King Anton, and the army of Ufficiali had surrounded us. Queen Leto's bright green eyes gleamed with satisfaction. She rubbed her hand along the curve of her bulging stomach and laughed a malicious laugh. King Anton smirked and my body went limp. My body crashed onto the floor with a large *THUD* and my mouth filled with a strange, metallic taste that I recognized as blood. I tried to move my limbs but was as if my muscles had turned off. I could only blink and breathe and. . . a sharp pain burst in my skull as I remembered the state of my body in the vision.

"The kingdom will finally be free." commented Queen Leto. "We can kill them now, but no. I think they deserve a more. . . amusing death. Guards! Take them to the dungeons!"

Oliver Hall

The cold was unbearable. Every inch of my skin was frozen, every muscle was hardened with ice, and my blood had turned to a solid.

At least, that's what I felt like.

My eyes slowly adjusted to the darkness and I could see the silhouettes of the people around me. Luna, Bella, Esme, Oscar, and Sam were all walking around the cell, their footsteps making synchronized taps against the stone floor.

I could feel the evil presence all around us. It was as if the King and Queen were in the cell with us. The evil that lay in their stone hearts was mirrored with what I felt. If the people around me were full of malice, then I felt like every inch of my body was slowly turning to ice. It was the other way around when I was around nice and thoughtful people. But even my friend's energies couldn't help me melt the ice around me.

I stood up and looked around. From what I could see, there was another person in the cell with us. The figure didn't move or talk, it just stood there. Chills froze my whole body. Who is that? And why is it just standing there? Not moving, not talking... To my right was a wall in which dozens of inscriptions were visible. Some read, *Help me*, while others just had initials or names. Whatever the case, the people that were here knew that there was no escaping. So they inscribed their names or messages into the walls of this filthy cell in order to be remembered.

"We need to get out of here." said Luna, the sudden determination in her voice told me that she knew it was hopeless, too. Or did she?

"But how?" asked Esme.

"Do you guys really think there's an exit to this place?" I asked, annoyed that they still had hopes of escaping. "It's hopeless."

"So you're just going to give up and die?" asked Sam.

"We're not going to die." said Bella.

"How do you know?" I asked. "Did you see it in one of your visions?"

"No, but--"

"We're just going to get out of here." said Oscar.

"Good luck finding an exit." I muttered, as I sat back down. What were they thinking? Everything was so hopeless. There was a reason the King and Queen put us in this cell. There. Was. No. Exit.

"There is an exit." said a familiar voice. I looked over to see where the voice came from, before realizing that the still figure belonged to Elina.

"Elina?" asked Sam, his voice full of caution.

"The vents. You could climb through them to get to the dumpsters." said Elina.

"Do you know someone who escaped this way?" I muttered.

"Oliver James Hall. Stop being so pessimistic!"

"Stop being so optimistic, Esme! Don't scold me for telling you guys the truth."

"Oliver! You-"

"Stop!" ordered Luna. "I can hear their thoughts. The King and Queen are close. We better get through those vents before they come. Elina, where did you say they were?" I asked. "And how about you? Come with us."

"No. I'll stay. You go."

After a lot of climbing, grunting, and cursing everyone was up in that vent. The only remnants of my friends' escape was the vent which was banged up and open.

"C'mon Oliver," ushered Esme from inside the vent. Her voice echoed, and it sounded a million miles away. I missed her already.

"No." I said, my voice hard as stone. "It's hopeless. You'll get caught. I'll stay with Elina."

I looked over at Elina and smiled. I respected her decision of staying in the cell. She wasn't stupid. She knew we would get caught if we tried to escape.

"No! Oliver! Please! Oli-"

Esme's cries were cut off as Luna's hand covered her mouth.

"They're coming." whispered Luna. She looked at me for a second as if to say, *Are you sure?* I nodded and turned away for I knew if I looked at Esme's wide purple eyes once more I would begin to sob uncontrollably. I slowly closed the vent, careful as not to make any sound. If there was a chance of my friends succeeding I wanted them to have it. But unfortunately I knew that they would die trying to escape death.

I heard the royal family's nearing footsteps and shivered. Maybe I would see Esme again. We would meet in heaven one day. We would have all we needed there. And maybe, just maybe if we were good enough during our lives, then maybe we would be reunited with our parents.

24 hours later

<h1 style="text-align: center;">Queen Leto</h1>

How could they? Little rascals! How could they find the one vent in the cell and escape? How could they humiliate me in such way? I had the pleasure of killing the traitor and one of the gifted twins but that didn't comfort me. I knew that there were five other gifted children running around Spero, threatening to destroy everything I had built so far. I stormed into my chambers and slammed the door behind me.

How could they?

I screamed with rage, but then stopped. This couldn't be good for Cedrica. I looked down at my bulging stomach and sighed. If I hadn't killed all my husband's lovers, then Cedrica wouldn't be first in line for the throne. But why did it have to be this way? Why couldn't my husband be faithful? Why couldn't Cedrica be his first child? Why couldn't I be his only love?

I knew the answers to all these questions, of course. I wasn't good enough for Anton. I wasn't that pretty or that smart. The only thing I had was wealth. Which brought me to this.

My eyes scanned the room and the ornate objects no longer felt needed. I didn't need silk curtains, marble floors, and golden picture frames. I needed love.

I stood up and walked over to a drawer. To the Forbidden Drawer. I needed to see Astoria once more. I opened the drawer and was surprised to see that Astoria's locket wasn't anywhere to be seen. I sighed and picked up a photograph inscribed with memories. In it, Astoria was on a swing, her platinum blonde hair fluttering behind her. Her emerald green eyes were filled to the brim with happiness as she rose higher and higher into the air. Her strapless pale pink gown was in soft waves as the soft breeze ruffled it up. But behind all this was something else.

Astoria walked into the park where I stood; her beautiful hair let down in a waterfall braid. She wore a strapless pale pink gown and cream colored stilettos that I knew Mother wouldn't approve of. She had a smile on her face as she eyed my own outfit.

"You know Mother won't approve of that." I said, as I tried to keep the jealousy to a minimum. How could Astoria look so good in that? How come she had the needed curves to fill the dress when I didn't?

"Relax, Leto." chided Astoria as she looked around. "Mom isn't going to see me anyway. She is, ahh, arranging your marriage to Prince Anton."

I was speechless. Me, marrying Prince Anton? Surely it was a joke. I mean, I knew that I would have to marry young. I knew that I would have to marry someone important, such as and aristocrat or an Adioutor. After all, I was a Lady, the daughter of a Duchess. But never have I ever expected to marry Prince Anton when I was seventeen.

"You must be joking," I stammered.

"No, actually. I'm quite serious," said Astoria. "You're going to meet him later today so you might want to change out of that."

I looked down at my own gown, not quite sure what was the problem with it. It was just how Mother liked it. A beautiful soft grey gown with long sleeves and and a high neckline. Covered up, just like a young woman should be.

"You look like someone died." muttered Astoria.

"I look just how Mother wants us to look. At least I'm not showing off my body with a strapless thing!"

"Tell me, do you enjoy being all covered up in the middle of summer when all the other girls wear short, strapless things? C'mon Leto! You know you despise it."

"Unlike you, Astoria, I strive to be a proper Lady. I will represent our family and will make Mother and Father proud!"

"Okay. Whatever you wish, My Lady." said Astoria as she bowed. "Just so you know, you're living a lie."

I considered this for a moment and knew that for once, Astoria was right. All the smiles I had to give random Dukes, Earls, and Viscounts were a lie. I knew that all the royal meetings and balls were a lie. And I *was living a lie because of my parents' social status. But I could do nothing about it. I couldn't even choose who to marry.*

Astoria headed over to one of the tire swings hanging from the branch of a plastic oak tree. She smiled and started swinging higher and higher, her laughter sending chills down my spine. How could Astoria be so free? She didn't care what others thought of her. She didn't care about Mother's rules and Father's punishments. She was living the life she wanted to live. And she could do this because she was prettier, smarter, braver, more athletic, skinnier. . . Astoria was more of everything good. She would probably marry a Duke, have strong children while living her life. She would be happy. I on the other hand, would have to follow royal protocols, I would have to pretend to love a prince that I didn't even like that much, and I would have to pretend to be happy as I carried his children.

And for whatever reason I felt as if I needed to capture Astoria in this moment. I rummaged through my leather handbag and took out a royal camera. It was the perfect size for my hands. Perfect for the perfect moment. I hid behind the plastic oak tree and took a picture of Astoria. It was perfect. Priceless. One day I would remember this and smile. After all, under all the jealousy there was love. I truly loved my little sister. But love could be temporary.

I sighed as I put the picture back in the drawer. I missed Astoria. I really did. But Astoria threatened the expansion of my kingdom. Therefore, she had to be eliminated. And I did so...

I rummaged through the drawer once again, desperate to find the locket that I gave Astoria for her thirteenth birthday. I wanted to see the other picture of us. I wanted to see her poem and my message. I needed to see the only thing that was left of Astoria.

After hours of rummaging through the whole room, I gave up. I fell onto the soft bed and closed my eyes, exhaustion creeped up on me. Just as I was relaxing, I heard the door creaking open. I stood up, panicked for I knew that this wasn't Anton. He never came in quietly. The door slowly opened and the room temperature dropped several degrees. A bone-chilling sensation settled in my body as an electric current ran down my spine. I tried to reach out for someone's energy, thinking that if this was a servant, I could manipulate her to make her go away. Instead, I was greeted with emptiness that numbed my brain.

A soft light came into the room, and I realized that the lights had gone out. I was tempted to scream but couldn't bring myself to. This was someone familiar. The soft light was so dim, it was almost transparent but I could still make out the thin outline of a girl. I could see her platinum blonde hair and emerald green eyes. The figure wore a pale dress that contrasted with the dark stain in her abdominal area. The dark liquid oozed out of her like a slow, lazy waterfall. It evaporated once it hit the floor but it never stopped oozing. All this made me want to vomit.

The girl smiled that same smile that I was used to seeing as a kid and thought I knew this all along, the reality of it settled in my uneasy stomach just now. Astoria. She came back to haunt me. Just like I thought she would. But why did it take her six years to come back?

"*Leto,*" said Astoria's ghost, in a sad voice that made me want to punch her. "*Why, Leto?*"

"You know why, Astoria." I said, careful as not to meet the ghost's eyes. "I highly doubt you miss your life in Spero."

"*I didn't like life in Spero because of you.*" said Astoria's ghost. The light flickered and I knew that Astoria's ghost was too weak to stay for long periods of time. Good. That would preserve my sanity. "*Think about it, Leto. Why did you do this to me?*"

The light vanished and I was left in the dark. The freezing temperatures and the uneasy feeling didn't vanish, though, and something told me that even though Astoria's ghost had vanished, her presence hadn't. She was still here in this room, haunting me for what I did six years ago. I took in a deep breath as I my hand traced the curve of my protruding stomach.

"Astoria," I said, making an effort to keep my voice steady. "Take what you want and leave."

I heard a high-pitched cackle that came from nowhere in particular. Astoria's presence wasn't just contained in a space, it was everywhere. It was all around me. A glass vase shattered somewhere in the room and that's when I realized that maybe Astoria wanted revenge. Maybe she wanted my life.

Esme Hall

"Luna Russell! We have to-"

"No, Esme. I know you're upset. We all are, but going back would be like commiting suicide!" said Luna, her ice blue eyes projecting fear that was enough to make me restrain myself. Luna wanted us to succeed in escaping the King and Queen, but she knew that unless we stayed quiet we would die.

"Please Luna," I pleaded, my desperation growing by the second. It had been nearly twenty-four hours since I last saw Oliver. There could still be a chance of him being alive. I couldn't just give up on my brother like that. I couldn't. We survived the fire that destroyed our childhood, we survived the orphanage, and we survived the Mortemisis outbreak. And all the time we stayed together. We couldn't just give up and split up now. "You guys don't have to go with me. I just need to see Oliver. I need to bring him back."

Luna looked at me with pity. She shook her head and closed her eyes.

"I'm sorry, Esme. But we both know he's dead."

"But even if he wasn't, he just gave up. You know you won't be able to convince him to come back. He gave up. There's nothing you can do about it." said Sam.

"But we could at least do something instead of just stay in this . . . shed." I said, wrinkling my nose in disgust. We'd traveled all through the night just to get to this forgotten storage shed in the outskirts of the city. I looked around. There was a single candle that floated in midair. The melted wax that dripped from the candle evaporated once it hit the wooden floor. The shed itself was crammed with lawn mowers, axes, shovels, buckets, rags, pickaxes, and other unnameable tools. We were all squished, making sleep impossible.

Luna looked around, taking in everything. Her ice blue eyes landed on each and every one of us. Her eyes scanned the room filled with various instruments and passed over the rickety walls that threatened to fall over at the slightest gust of wind. Luna drew her knees to her chest and started sobbing, her bony shoulders trembling.

Bella rushed over to Luna, and started comforting her. Oscar soon joined them. Then Sam. I immediately felt like a total idiot for not thinking about Luna. No one wanted this. It was hard on all of us.

"I'm sorry." wailed Luna. "I didn't want any of this to happen. I just. . . I just didn't want to die like that. I'm sorry!"

"Luna, it's. . . it's not your fault." I stammered, as I scrambled over to her trembling body. "Please don't cry. It's. . . it's okay."

Luna continued to sob and we let for we knew that she needed it. Sometimes it's better to sob than to hide all those emotions inside you. At least, that's what my mother used to say. My mother. My beautiful mother.

I hugged my knees to my chest as I cried. Huge water splotches appeared on my tights, ruining the beige color. Why did this have to happen, to me? Why did Demi Lucas have to pick on me? I hadn't done anything!

I heard the door open and I squinted through the kaleidoscope of tears that appeared before my eyes in order to see the intruder. My mother came in, her beautiful lavender colored silk skirt making soft waves around her ankles. She straightened her white cashmere blouse as she sat down next to me, the soft hand rubbing calming patterns on my back.

We sat there for a while, not daring to say anything. Finally, my mother spoke up.

"What happened, Esme?" she said, in a soft voice that sent chills down my spine.

I stayed silent for a while, not sure if I should tell her absolutely everything or if I should spare her some details. My mother just sat there, patiently waiting for my answer.

"I lost Oliver, mom! He just gave up and stayed in the cell.
He, he . . . Oh mom, my heart hurts so much!"

"I understand my dear. Please know he is in a better place now. I'll let you cry. Sometimes it's better to cry than to let the emotions poison you. It's better if you let your emotions show rather than hide them inside."

My mother walked out of the room, and I cried even harder. She didn't understand. She never would. But I loved her either way. She would always be my beautiful mother.

Luna's continuous sobs broke up the flashback and I remembered that I was still in the storage shed, trapped as the King and Queen of Spero sent people to hunt us down.

"Let her be." I muttered, loud enough for Bella, Sam, and Oscar to hear. Luna looked up, her face red and puffy, the tears leaving trails behind them as they sped down her gentle face. "Sometimes it's better to cry."

Sam Grey

Esme turned around to fidget with the various instruments in the shed, her bony back facing us. *Sometimes it's better to cry*. Sure, I guess. But it always felt good to have people that care about you supporting you through your moments of crisis. Support meant that people cared about you, that you were loved. Not many people have that nowadays.

Luna shuddered as her sobs came to a stop. She wiped her soaking face in her shirt and stood up, her bony legs wobbling beneath her

"We have to leave." said Luna, her ice blue eyes scanning each person in the room to make sure we all got the message. She opened the door and stepped outside, the darkness of the night swallowing her. I looked over at Oscar. His eyes were glassy once again, and I wondered what was going on in his head. Esme walked outside, followed by Bella, her once beautiful blonde hair now tangled up and matted with sweat and blood. Oscar stood up to follow Bella, and I realized that I was the only one left in the musty storage shed. I stood up and walked to the doorway, now aware of the faint thundering of footsteps in the distance. Someone was coming. And we needed to get out of here. Like now.

Oscar Smith

We followed Luna for a long time, the darkness swallowing her up and making her impossible to see if we got only a few feet from each other. Billions of stars gleamed in the night sky each twinkling with its own tempo. A shooting star sprinted across the dark sky and I made a silent wish that we would get out of this mess. Alive. But superstitions and wishes were probably not enough to save us from reality. We were the most hunted people in all of Spero, right now. Getting out of here would be a miracle. I looked up to the sky, once again awe-struck by the fact that instead of a silvery moon, there was a large green planet in the night sky. It covered only some of the sky but it was quite large. Or so it seemed.

"Are we there yet?" asked Sam. He reminded me of a little kid. Of Gabrielle. I swallowed down the grief and pain that quickly resurfaced and I focused on the night sky. "Let me rephrase my question. Where are we going?"

Luna turned around, half of her face obscured by her hair.

"Away from civilization. That's where we're going."

"That's cool," answered Sam. "It's a great plan. We'll die slowly and painfully away from civilization. No one will help us."

"No, we won't." said Bella, finally speaking up. "We won't. I can see that we'll live. I saw a glimpse of. . . an event. It's probably going to happen today. Maybe, tomorrow. But we were alive so we won't die. . . now."

"See?" I said. "We can do this. We won't die."

"Okay. Whatever." muttered Sam.

We continued walking for what seemed like ages. Suddenly, a shrill scream pierced the still night air. The high-pitched noise sent cold chills creeping down my spine and I knew that we weren't the only ones here. I looked at Luna, praying to an invisible god that she was okay.

Luna's ice blue eyes widened with horror. She was checked that everyone was still here. Sam? Check. Esme? Check. Bella?

Wait. Where was Bella?

The tall grass made soft waves in the midnight breeze, making it impossible to see who had caused the bone-chilling scream. The person screamed again, and a horrible realization settled in my gut.

Luna looked at me once again, her eyes wider than marbles. Fear had sprouted all over her, from her trembling knees to her pale face, it was everywhere. I looked at Esme, not surprised to see her in a similar state. Sam was pale but wasn't shaking. I. . . well I don't know what I was. Three figures appeared in the distance, their silhouettes barely visible in the dark midnight sky. Two of the figures walked with confidence, while the third was struggling and squirming. It took me a moment to realize that this. . . was bad. Really bad.

"And we meet again." said a high-pitched voice that sounded awfully familiar. "You can't save yourselves from what's meant to be."

My heart dropped to my knees as I reality settled in.

Esme whimpered.

"It's. . . it's. . . "

"The Queen," I finished.

Luna Russell

I looked over at Oscar, fear washing over me. Oscar looked back, our eyes locking. For a moment, I thought there was something special in the way he looked at me. Something. . . different. But that quickly vanished. His glassy eyes were replaced with a hard, stern stare, and I knew that I had failed him. I had failed him. And Bella. And Sam. And Esme. I was the one that led the group through the night. I was the one who heard the evil thoughts and thought that we could escape them. I was the one that decided not to tell the rest of the group for fear of injecting panic and chaos. And now, everything was my fault. Everything.

Esme whimpered once again.

"*Nunc*!" yelled the King, the fact that his order was in a foreign language making me feel blind and useless. The Ufficiali moved forward, their footsteps, quick, light, and almost silent. Their muscular arms yanked our hands behind our backs and we fell to our knees. I felt useless, like a doll on strings controlled by the King and Queen's pets.

"You know, I'm considering your deaths." mused the Queen, as she held the squirming figure that I was now sure was Bella. "I'm wondering if I should do this the clean way. It won't be very. . . amusing, but it will be merciful."

Esme started squirming, her body trying to shake off the intruder. The guard snarled as he pushed her down, grunting with effort as he tried to keep her down.

"But maybe we could be messy." said Queen Leto in a faraway but amused tone. "Maybe your deaths could be. . . amusing. Ufficiali! Take them to the palace grounds. Everyone shall see this!"

I woke up as we were pulling into Spero's main city. My head felt heavy as if it was about to explode. My eyelids felt swollen and I could barely open my eyes. My limbs felt as if the muscles had turned off. Overall, I felt useless.

"Your Majesty, the fragile one woke up." said one of the Ufficiali. I looked around, surprised to see that my hands were behind my back, my skinny wrists being held by the Ufficiali's large hands. I didn't remember falling asleep. Or being knocked out.

I heard a muffled *pop* and it was as if someone had turned the lights back on. The spell, or whatever it was, broke and I suddenly had a lot of energy. I could now feel the pain that settled deep in my bones. The pain, it was everywhere. But so was my energy. I felt as if I could run miles without getting tired. My head no longer felt as if it was about to explode and my eyelids no longer felt heavy. The muscles in my limbs turned on. I was alive and full of energy.

"Good, good. Let her go, Gullery."

Gullery. . . the name sounded familiar but. . . . how could this be? Abbyson Gullery was an Earthen. But he wouldn't possibly agree to serve for the Queen.

Unless. . .

The tight grip on my wrists loosened and I turned around frantically, searching for my friends. Sam, Oscar, and Esme were next to me in a similar state. Esme's large purple eyes searched around the carriage, her face face pale and frantic. Sam tried to look calm but, failed to hide the fear that plagued his insides. Oscar looked fierce, his blue eyes hard, his jaw set, and his breathing hard. He looked ready for battle. And Bella. . . was nowhere to be seen.

We pulled onto the main palace road. The Queen chuckled and I found myself growling, the fierce noise escaping through my mouth. The Queen chuckled once again, the sound of her pleasure igniting a fire in my chest.

"Why?" whispered Sam, his usual platinum blond hair now light brown and matted with sweat and dust. Sure, gifted like us healed quickly on Spero but blood or severe pain didn't disappear that fast. "Why are we going to the palace? Why didn't they just kill us there, in the field?"

I thought about what the royal family was trying to do, before an idea came to mind. If the royal family was doing what I thought they were doing. . . then maybe we could escape. Maybe-

Bella Atherton

I wandered the barren field, searching for my friends. Searching for a sign of civilization. But there was nothing. Absolutely nothing. Just knee-length grass that tugged on my ripped jeans.

There was a soft breeze running through the field, it's chilly tentacles embracing my body. I shivered as another gust of wind blew through. The treacherous night had passed and a faint Lux gleamed overhead. And although it was visible, and although it shone with light, it projected no comforting warmth whatsoever.

I felt another sharp pain in the soles of my feet followed by warm liquid that oozed around in my shoes. I sighed, knowing that yet another blister had popped.

I wandered the field, my thoughts roaming along with me. Last night was horrid. I remember being at the back of the group, Sam's hair being the only thing I could see. A short vision plagued me at the time, but it had been nothing important. Or so I had thought.

The vision had portrayed all of us roaming through a barren field. It was dark and breezy, the soft gusts of wind making the dry blades of grass irritate our exposed shins. We wandered the fields aimlessly, lost as we wandered the fields, looking for something to help us escape from Spero.

But we were already wandering about aimlessly although Luna guided us through the night, I knew very well that she did not know where we were going. Or why we were going there. We were lost, and we all knew it.

I sighed, knowing that I better hurry if I want to save my friends. Surely they were with the King and Queen, captured and terrified. The mere thought of losing my friends to that witch made me choke on a sob. A sob filled with anger and despair for I couldn't lose yet another person. I'd lost my mom and Evelyn to Mortemisis. I'd lost Cara long ago when she decided she was too good for us. I'd lost Aunt Malena to leukemia. I'd lost Lauren at the palace, and was sure that she was now dead. And now I was losing my friends.

I squinted at the horizon, trying to find something that could lead me back to Spero's main city. My friends were at the palace. I was sure of that.

A couple hundred meters away, I spotted a large pole with signs on each side of it. A pole. That wasn't something you found in nature. Meaning that someone had put it up there. Someone. And that someone was part of civilization.

I sprinted to the pole, my eyes never leaving my destination. My lungs felt like shriveled plastic bags, the oxygen going through my nose stung my nostrils, and my eyes watered up. My arms felt like rubber and my feet ached as I pushed them to run faster and faster and faster and. . .

Everything went black.

Esme Hall

I stumbled as the guards pushed me forward, making me stumble and trip on my own feet. The guard's hands dug into my flesh, making the pain race up and down my body. Somewhere beside me Sam grunted with effort as he tried to pull away from the guard.

I closed my eyes for a moment, wishing that Bella was with us. She would be able to tell what would happen to us. She would know if we would die. But Bella was gone. Dead. Or so we believed. The Queen never told us what they did with Bella. She would just flash us that malicious smile of hers that made my insides burn with hatred.

If only. If only.

The guards pushed us around until we got to a dimly lit room. The room was freezing and the marble floor suddenly turned to stone. Death lingered in the air, and I felt a bone-chilling gust of air blow into my face.

The King issued a command, and the pressure against my arms loosened. I fell onto the cold floor, the impact making me bite my tongue. A warm, metallic taste filled my mouth and I had the urge to spit the blood out. I swallowed instead, though. I would not give the Queen the satisfaction of my blood. Of my pain. No. I would not.

The blood that I had swallowed irritated my empty stomach, and I felt dizzy and lightheaded, my body ready to puke out the foreign contents I had swallowed. But no. I held myself together, willing for the royal family to leave us in the cell. To leave us alone so that I could help myself.

"Oh, this is going to be so much fun." mused the Queen, as she rubbed her hand along the curve of her bulging stomach. Oh, how I wanted to punch her evil smiling face! Not that I had anything against pregnant women or developing babies, but something about the Queen's smug satisfaction made the dark thoughts spring up like seedlings. "And it is too bad that I must go into a meeting now. But soon, I shall have my fun and entertainment. Until then, *ciao!*"

The Queen spun around, leaving us in the darkness of the cell. I could hear her footsteps get farther and farther until I could hear them no more. I sucked in a surge of air and held my breath. I didn't know why I was doing it. I just was. I held my breath until my head felt like it was about to explode. Until my lungs screamed for air. Until I could hear the pumping of my heart slowly start to fade.

I exhaled, my breaths coming in short, raspy gasps. I saw Sam looking at me as if I was crazy but I couldn't care less. I rubbed my arms, my fingers gently pressing against the painful dents the guard's hands had made. I looked over at my friends taking in their matted hair, dirty faces, and skinny bodies. Just then, the temperature in the room dropped by a couple degrees, the cold air now freezing. Everyone's eyes widened and I knew that they felt the change in temperature as well.

Sam and Oscar shifted uncomfortably and Luna's mouth opened in a silent scream. I just stood there, frozen.

"You can escape, you know." said a soft voice, belonging to a girl. I looked around frantically, searching for the source of the voice. The cold was unbearable now, and I couldn't stop myself from shivering. A soft buzzing sound in my ears, like jumbled whispers that I couldn't shut out. The buzzing was louder now, more frantic, but I couldn't hear anything specific. It was just a jumble of whispers. . .

A dim light appeared in the corner of the cell, the light barely reaching over to where we were. The light moved in a slow manner, and I realized that this was the figure of a girl. This was a ghost. The ghost girl made her way over to us, the light of her aura brighter as she neared us. I could now see her platinum blonde hair and the silver crown that rested on her head. She wore a pale dress that had no exact color to describe it, the dress fluttering around as she floated over to us. The girl was beautiful, possibly one of the most beautiful girls I had ever seen, but that beauty was ruined once you looked down at her abdomen. The dark stain glared at me, as it slowly dripped, the drops of blood evaporating once they hit the dungeon floor. The girl looked awfully familiar. Like. . . like. . .

The static buzzing of whispers in my head got louder and louder, until it was unbearable.

"You don't have to be my sister's guinea pigs." said the girl. My eyes widened. Her sister? Queen Leto was her sister? *"But you can't escape unless you claim your true identities."*

"Who are you?" asked Oscar, as he stepped back, slowly inching farther and farther from the ghost girl.

"Astoria Ferelle Hale, Leto Hale's younger sister." said the girl, a sad smile painted on her face. *"Haven't you heard of me?"* asked Astoria's ghost, as she tilted her head. *"I shouldn't be surprised, though. Leto likes to keep me a secret. Anyway. . . I'm going to help you escape from my sister's claws."*

We all stood there frozen, not knowing what to, not knowing what to say, not knowing how to react in general. Queen Leto had a younger sister? That's. . .

"Now listen," said Astoria's ghost. *"Long ago there were Eleven Elders of Spero. Eleven Elders, each one of them had a supernatural power that was out of the ordinary. Leonas the Forty-Third could read minds. Like your little Luna girl. Yosif Kukk could see the future, like your missing girl. Bogdan Sylvester would know a person's life story with just a touch. Fynn Carr would get surges of hot and cold whenever he was around certain people. Karla Rebane could project forcefields of energy to block one's manipulation."*

Luna shuddered, but didn't say anything. Next to her, Sam and Oscar sat perfectly still. I looked around the dark room, confused. Was I going crazy? I mean, surely sane people didn't see the ghosts of the Queen's younger sister. Sane people wouldn't see talking ghosts at all.

"Dolores Lynch could see people's auras and Lythande Silva was immune to mental manipulation. Josef Khan had manipulation ten times stronger than the average person. Zelda Liu could hear what people were saying, whether it was people on Fidem or people on Earth. She knew everything." Astoria's ghost paused. *"Her twin sister Fera Liu could see everything. Rachel Vane could tell when someone was lying to her. She always knew."*

Astoria's ghost paused, her lips forming a tight line.

"The furies of Spero, though, rebelled, for they wanted a monarchy. All Eleven Elders had to escape from Spero, for furies were starting to get violent. They couldn't accept the fact that the Elders were different. They didn't have manipulation as a gift. Instead, they had supernatural powers." continued the ghost. *"The Elders were lead by Zelda and Frau, who helped the Elders escape to Earth. Down on Earth, the Elders were normal. They were no longer connected to power of Spero. The power that came from inside the planet. They were normal. Like Earthens."*

"Why are you telling us this?" I asked. I mean, the Eleven Elders barely seemed to connect with us. Sure, some of us had the same powers as them, but otherwise we weren't alike.

"Listen," prompted Astoria's ghost. *"The Elven Elders interacted with Earthens and soon they all had offspring. It's time to claim your identities."*

"You are descended from the Eleven Elders."

Luna Russell

"Wait, what?" I asked, making sense of the words Astoria's ghost had said.

"*You are descended from the Eleven Elders.*" repeated the ghost of Astoria, her voice monotone. "*And so are eleven other children. Though four did die. Oliver Hall, Valeena Larson, Liza King, and Jo Sparks, I think. Anyway you must meet up with those other kids. The Gifted Kids that are alive. That's the only way to save yourselves from fate.*"

"Wait! How are we supposed to find two other kids?" asked Oscar, but Astoria's light was now gone. Darkness engulfed the room and the temperature rose by a couple degrees. I hadn't realized that Astoria's ghost was gone. We were alone. All alone.

We had to escape. We had to go to a place. And we had to meet up with some other people. But how exactly were we supposed to do this?

"Eleven Elders," muttered Esme, as she turned to look at us. "What now?"

I looked up at the ceiling for once not knowing what to do.

About the Author

Magdalina Goranova enjoys reading fiction books. That was the main inspiration behind her decision to write this story. "Blackout" is the first book of a trilogy.

Magi is a middle school student. She was born in the beautiful Rockies of Colorado and still lives there. Besides reading, she also enjoys drawing, acting and climbing.